TOEIC

練習測驗（10）

聽力錄音QR碼（1~100題）

U0084649

LISTENING TEST

In the Listening test, you will be asked to demonstrate how well you understand spoken English. The entire Listening test will last approximately 45 minutes. There are four parts, and directions are given for each part. You must mark your answers on the separate answer sheet. Do not write your answers in your test book.

PART 1

Directions: For each question in this part, you will hear four statements about a picture in your test book. When you hear the statements, you must select the one statement that best describes what you see in the picture. Then find the number of the question on your answer sheet and mark your answer. The statements will not be printed in your test book and will be spoken only one time.

Statement (C), "They're sitting at a table," is the best description of the picture, so you should select answer (C) and mark it on your answer sheet.

1.

2.

GO ON TO THE NEXT PAGE.

3.

4.

5.

6.

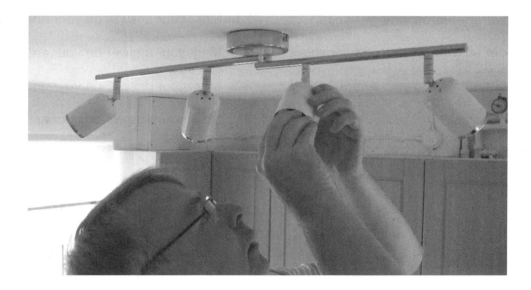

GO ON TO THE NEXT PAGE.

PART 2

Directions: You will hear a question or statement and three responses spoken in English. They will not be printed in your test book and will be spoken only one time. Select the best response to the question or statement and mark the letter (A), (B), or (C) on your answer sheet.

7. Mark your answer on your answer sheet.

8. Mark your answer on your answer sheet.

9. Mark your answer on your answer sheet.

10. Mark your answer on your answer sheet.

11. Mark your answer on your answer sheet.

12. Mark your answer on your answer sheet.

13. Mark your answer on your answer sheet.

14. Mark your answer on your answer sheet.

15. Mark your answer on your answer sheet.

16. Mark your answer on your answer sheet.

17. Mark your answer on your answer sheet.

18. Mark your answer on your answer sheet.

19. Mark your answer on your answer sheet.

20. Mark your answer on your answer sheet.

21. Mark your answer on your answer sheet.

22. Mark your answer on your answer sheet.

23. Mark your answer on your answer sheet.

24. Mark your answer on your answer sheet.

25. Mark your answer on your answer sheet.

26. Mark your answer on your answer sheet.

27. Mark your answer on your answer sheet.

28. Mark your answer on your answer sheet.

29. Mark your answer on your answer sheet.

30. Mark your answer on your answer sheet.

31. Mark your answer on your answer sheet.

PART 3

Directions: You will hear some conversations between two people. You will be asked to answer three questions about what the speakers say in each conversation. Select the best response to each question and mark the letter (A), (B), (C), or (D) on your answer sheet. The conversation will not be printed in your test book and will be spoken only one time.

32. Where does the man work?
  (A) At a police station.
  (B) At a school library.
  (C) At a transportation company.
  (D) At a theater.

33. What does the man ask about?
  (A) When a meeting will start.
  (B) Where a business is located.
  (C) How many visitors are expected.
  (D) How the bill will be paid.

34. What will the man prepare?
  (A) Informational brochures.
  (B) Name badges.
  (C) Training manuals.
  (D) An expense report.

35. What is the purpose of the telephone call?
  (A) To arrange a delivery.
  (B) To request an upgrade.
  (C) To place an order.
  (D) To confirm a reservation.

36. What does the man say is required?
  (A) A passport.
  (B) A credit card.
  (C) A signature.
  (D) A security code.

37. Who does the woman say she will call?
  (A) Her lawyer.
  (B) Her boss.
  (C) Her husband.
  (D) Her neighbor.

38. Where are the speakers?
  (A) At a shoe store.
  (B) At a print shop.
  (C) At a dry cleaner.
  (D) At a restaurant.

39. Why is the man at the restaurant?
  (A) To return some equipment.
  (B) To pick up some samples.
  (C) To look for a missing item.
  (D) To discuss a catering order.

40. What does Rachel ask about?
  (A) A price.
  (B) A color.
  (C) A location.
  (D) A name.

41. Why is the man calling?
  (A) To confirm payment information.
  (B) To request customer feedback.
  (C) To offer a free consultation.
  (D) To reschedule an installation.

42. What caused a delay?
  (A) An appointment was missed.
  (B) A product was temporarily unavailable.
  (C) Some equipment was faulty.
  (D) Some forms were misplaced.

43. What does the man say he will do?
  (A) Send some product samples.
  (B) Inspect some merchandise.
  (C) Pass on some information.
  (D) Issue a refund.

GO ON TO THE NEXT PAGE.

44. Where are the speakers?
   (A) At a university library.
   (B) At a train station.
   (C) At a fitness center.
   (D) At a sports stadium.

45. Why does the woman need to verify her residency?
   (A) To vote in an election.
   (B) To make a reservation.
   (C) To verify her date of birth.
   (D) To receive a discount.

46. What will the woman most likely do next?
   (A) Complete some paperwork.
   (B) Make an online payment.
   (C) Speak to a manager.
   (D) Sign a lease.

47. What are the speakers working on?
   (A) A bottle design.
   (B) A tax audit.
   (C) An advertising budget.
   (D) A training manual.

48. What does the man say about the company softball team?
   (A) The team is receiving an award.
   (B) The team is participating in a competition.
   (C) The players are male and female.
   (D) The players are getting new uniforms.

49. Why does the woman say, "I think we can spare you for a couple of hours on Friday"?
   (A) To extend an approaching deadline.
   (B) To disagree with a colleague's opinion.
   (C) To approve the man's request.
   (D) To express dissatisfaction with the client's request.

50. Why did the woman want to meet with the man?
   (A) To follow up on a job offer.
   (B) To congratulate the man on a nomination.
   (C) To return a favor.
   (D) To ask the man about his progress at work.

51. What does the man say he had trouble with?
   (A) Submitting a report.
   (B) Finding volunteers for a survey.
   (C) Formatting a website.
   (D) Receiving international shipments.

52. What does the woman suggest the man do?
   (A) Read a company handbook.
   (B) Participate in a training session.
   (C) Use a database.
   (D) Talk to a coordinator.

53. What is scheduled for April 17?
   (A) A board meeting.
   (B) A cooking demonstration.
   (C) A musical performance.
   (D) A fitness center reopening.

54. What does the man thank the woman for?
   (A) Creating a poster.
   (B) Revising a calendar.
   (C) Booking an artist.
   (D) Responding to a complaint.

55. What does the man say he will do?
   (A) Contact a print shop.
   (B) Listen to a recording.
   (C) Check a budget.
   (D) Update a schedule.

56. What has the woman recently done?
  (A) Led a product demonstration.
  (B) Attended a trade show.
  (C) Ordered business cards.
  (D) Submitted a proposal.

57. What does the man think the woman should do?
  (A) Write a review.
  (B) Buy a new camera.
  (C) Organize a party.
  (D) Use a phone application.

58. What does the man like about the premium version of a product?
  (A) It is easier to use.
  (B) It is the industry standard.
  (C) It has more storage space.
  (D) It comes with warranty.

59. Who most likely is the man?
  (A) A mechanic.
  (B) A lawyer.
  (C) A doctor.
  (D) A teacher.

60. Why does the woman say, "I sit at a desk for 10 hours a day"?
  (A) To request a second opinion.
  (B) To apologize for an error.
  (C) To describe her area of expertise.
  (D) To explain the cause of a problem.

61. What does the man recommend the woman do?
  (A) Rearrange her work space.
  (B) Put her name on a waiting list.
  (C) Join a fitness center.
  (D) Take breaks at certain intervals.

Radcliff Heights Community Center

Advanced Computer Classes

Session 1	Database Management	Mondays at 11:00 a.m.
Session 2	Network Security	Wednesdays at 5:30 p.m.
Session 3	Website Administration	Thursdays at 6:00 p.m.
Session 4	Website Administration	Saturdays at 1:00 p.m.

62. What was announced at the staff meeting?
  (A) A sales event will be held.
  (B) An employee will leave the company.
  (C) A merger will take place.
  (D) A new product will be launched.

63. What is the woman nervous about doing?
  (A) Applying for a job.
  (B) Taking an exam.
  (C) Being interviewed for an article.
  (D) Starting her own company.

64. Look at the graphic. Which session will the woman most likely attend?
  (A) Session 1.
  (B) Session 2.
  (C) Session 3.
  (D) Session 4.

GO ON TO THE NEXT PAGE.

Nibbler's Oceanview Restaurant
Daily Specials

Monday
Catch of the Day

Tuesday
Clam Chowder

Wednesday
Fish and Chips

Thursday
All You Can Eat Shrimp Buffet

Friday
Surf and Turf Platter

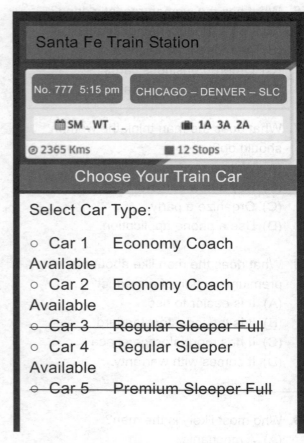

65. Look at the graphic. What day is the conversation taking place?
    (A) Tuesday.
    (B) Wednesday.
    (C) Thursday.
    (D) Friday.

66. What does the man ask about?
    (A) Outdoor seating.
    (B) Group discounts.
    (C) Catering services.
    (D) Vegetarian options.

67. Why does the woman apologize?
    (A) She cannot accept a coupon.
    (B) She cannot issue a refund.
    (C) A meal course was not delivered.
    (D) An area is closed for remodeling.

68. Why does the woman dislike Santa Fe train station?
    (A) It has no Internet access.
    (B) It is being renovated.
    (C) It is always understaffed.
    (D) It is inconveniently located.

69. Look at the graphic. Which car will the speakers most likely choose?
    (A) Car 1.
    (B) Car 2.
    (C) Car 3.
    (D) Car 4.

70. What does the woman ask the man about?
    (A) What time he wants to return.
    (B) Where he wants to meet.
    (C) How he wants to pay.
    (D) How much luggage he is bringing.

Directions: You will hear some talks given by a single speaker. You will be asked to answer three questions about what the speaker says in each talk. Select the best response to each question and mark the letter (A), (B), (C), or (D) on your answer sheet. The talks will not be printed in your test book and will be spoken only one time.

71. What industry do the managers work in?
    (A) Education.
    (B) Marketing.
    (C) Transportation.
    (D) Restaurant.

72. According to the speaker, what area of the business needs to be improved?
    (A) Personnel retention.
    (B) Staff recruitment.
    (C) Customer service.
    (D) Curriculum preparation.

73. What will the managers most likely do next?
    (A) Meet new students.
    (B) Submit student grade reports.
    (C) Conduct a training session.
    (D) Listen to a presentation.

74. What type of company does the speaker work for?
    (A) An electronics manufacturer.
    (B) A travel agency.
    (C) A hotel chain.
    (D) An accounting firm.

75. What does the speaker mention about the position?
    (A) It requires official certification.
    (B) It is in a newly established department.
    (C) It involves frequent travel.
    (D) It is a part-time position.

76. Why is the listener asked to return a call?
    (A) To provide a reference.
    (B) To negotiate a salary.
    (C) To schedule an interview.
    (D) To confirm a delivery.

77. What department do the listeners work in?
    (A) Maintenance.
    (B) Purchasing.
    (C) Information Technology.
    (D) Marketing.

78. What does the speaker say is available on a company website?
    (A) An employee directory.
    (B) A catalog.
    (C) A map.
    (D) A schedule.

79. What does the speaker ask the listeners to do at the next meeting?
    (A) Choose a logo.
    (B) Elect a representative.
    (C) Discuss their ideas.
    (D) Sign a document.

80. What is the speaker preparing to do?
    (A) Conduct a tour.
    (B) Organize a banquet.
    (C) Travel overseas.
    (D) Give a presentation.

81. What does the speaker request?
    (A) A copy of a contract.
    (B) Access to a network.
    (C) A list of guests.
    (D) A video screen.

82. Why does the speaker say, "I already hired a limousine service"?
    (A) To decline an offer.
    (B) To explain a procedure.
    (C) To request directions.
    (D) To propose a schedule change.

GO ON TO THE NEXT PAGE.

83. What kind of business do the listeners most likely work for?
    (A) A shoe manufacturer.
    (B) A landscaping firm.
    (C) A utility company.
    (D) A food and beverage distributor.

84. What is the purpose of the meeting?
    (A) To learn how to operate new equipment.
    (B) To discuss job openings.
    (C) To improve customer relations.
    (D) To review safety procedures.

85. Why does the man say, "I was pressed for time to get the materials together"?
    (A) To praise an employee.
    (B) To provide an excuse.
    (C) To accept an apology.
    (D) To change a deadline.

86. What kind of event is the speaker organizing?
    (A) A fund-raising marathon.
    (B) An annual company outing.
    (C) A building dedication.
    (D) A music festival.

87. What is the speaker's reason for calling?
    (A) To explain a recent change in policy.
    (B) To confirm the number of attendees.
    (C) To discuss the content of a performance.
    (D) To request a missing payment.

88. What does the speaker say about the event?
    (A) The admission fee has increased.
    (B) There is limited seating.
    (C) It will be held at a different location.
    (D) It will be well-attended.

89. According to the speaker, what took place this month?
    (A) A department training.
    (B) A product launch.
    (C) A company merger.
    (D) A budget review.

90. What is Norman Lee's field of expertise?
    (A) Electrical engineering.
    (B) Graphic design.
    (C) Organic chemistry.
    (D) International law.

91. What is Norman Lee currently doing?
    (A) Developing a project budget.
    (B) Visiting a factory.
    (C) Conducting an experiment.
    (D) Meeting with the board of directors.

92. What class does the speaker teach?
    (A) Graphic design.
    (B) Computer programming.
    (C) Martial arts.
    (D) Yoga.

93. Why does the speaker say, "We share this room with a meditation class"?
    (A) To invite students to another class.
    (B) To remind participants to watch their belongings.
    (C) To stress the importance of finishing on time.
    (D) To apologize for an inconvenient location.

94. What are the listeners reminded to do before they leave?
    (A) Replace their desks.
    (B) Pay for registration.
    (C) Take some handouts.
    (D) Provide some feedback.

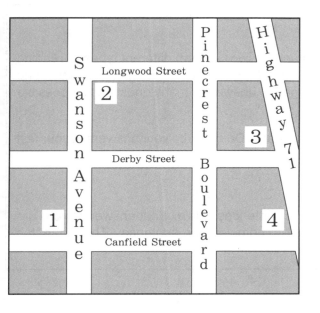

Checklist

1 _____
Check store number

2 _____
Match titles with invoice

3 _____
Inspect books for damage

4 _____
Move items to storeroom

95. What caused a problem?
(A) Building demolition.
(B) Bad weather.
(C) A train delay.
(D) An auto accident.

96. Look at the graphic. Which location is the speaker describing?
(A) Location 1.
(B) Location 2.
(C) Location 3.
(D) Location 4.

97. What does the speaker say will take place tomorrow?
(A) A grand opening.
(B) A race.
(C) A parade.
(D) A musical performance.

98. What does the speaker say he is concerned about?
(A) Wasted staff time.
(B) Customer complaints.
(C) Excessive absences.
(D) Limited storage space.

99. Look at the graphic. Which step does the speaker say requires special attention?
(A) Step 1.
(B) Step 2.
(C) Step 3.
(D) Step 4.

100. What does the speaker say is going to happen?
(A) A sales event will begin.
(B) A branch store will close.
(C) Fewer shipments will be sent out.
(D) More merchandise will arrive.

This is the end of the Listening test. Turn to Part 5 in your test book.

GO ON TO THE NEXT PAGE.

READING TEST

In the Reading test, you will read a variety of texts and answer several different types of reading comprehension questions. The entire Reading test will last 75 minutes. There are three parts, and directions are given for each part. You are encouraged to answer as many questions as possible within the time allowed.

You must mark your answers on the separate answer sheet. Do not write your answers in your test book.

PART 5

Directions: A word or phrase is missing in each of the sentences below. Four answer choices are given below each sentence. Select the best answer to complete the sentence. Then mark the letter (A), (B), (C), or (D) on your answer sheet.

101. More than a decade ago, Dean Lorber ------- a promising career in finance to join a start-up company.
(A) will leave
(B) was left
(C) leave
(D) left

102. On-going road construction on southbound Route 83 has ------- traffic delays at the Carlton Interchange.
(A) directed
(B) operated
(C) caused
(D) instructed

103. Mr. Wanshack requests that the research team e-mail the final report to ------- before 5:30 p.m.
(A) his
(B) himself
(C) him
(D) he

104. Geartex ------- sends e-mails with discount codes to customers who have registered for premium accounts.
(A) nearly
(B) often
(C) highly
(D) ever

105. All travel-related business expenses should be ------- to the accounting department.
(A) submitted
(B) submissions
(C) submit
(D) submits

106. Customers should contact the manufacturer ------- for any technical support.
(A) direct
(B) directing
(C) directly
(D) direction

107. Passengers must show both boarding passes and passports ------- boarding the plane.
(A) how
(B) when
(C) as
(D) if

108. One of the major challenges companies must deal with is maintaining employee -------.
(A) morale
(B) reality
(C) closure
(D) consequence

14

109. Seminar attendees at the Civic Center are reminded that roads in the vicinity are ------- crowded during peak hours.
(A) usually
(B) exactly
(C) finely
(D) cleanly

110. ------- his period of unemployment, Dylan applied to over a dozen law firms.
(A) Between
(B) During
(C) Behind
(D) From

111. Omega Airlines is expanding its regional flight coverage to maintain a ------- edge in the transportation marketplace.
(A) competition
(B) competitive
(C) competitively
(D) compete

112. Ms. Mathers laid out the marketing campaign before ------- sales figures prior to the campaign's launch.
(A) cooperating
(B) designing
(C) purchasing
(D) announcing

113. It is the project manager's responsibility to make sure that all custom products meet the client's -------.
(A) specific
(B) to specify
(C) specifically
(D) specifications

114. Passengers are reminded to stow their ------- baggage in the overhead compartments.
(A) unlimited
(B) personal
(C) accurate
(D) temporary

115. A merger of the two companies is one ------- outcome of the meeting between the two CEOs.
(A) possibilities
(B) possibly
(C) possible
(D) possibility

116. Please ------- all sections of the lease application and provide a signature where indicated.
(A) mature
(B) deliver
(C) terminate
(D) complete

117. At Concordia, the ------- has always been on building customer relationships, not on increasing profits.
(A) emphasis
(B) emphasize
(C) emphasized
(D) emphatic

118. ------- presenting a valid photo ID, customers may claim parcels from Allied Air Express.
(A) Upon
(B) Among
(C) Without
(D) Over

119. At a towering height of 1,400 feet, Willis Tower can be seen from ------- in the metropolitan area.
(A) absolutely
(B) around
(C) entirely
(D) anywhere

120. Mr. Jenkins suggests that we ------- the shipment until the order is complete.
(A) delay
(B) expire
(C) wait
(D) remain

GO ON TO THE NEXT PAGE.

121. All department supervisors are encouraged to familiarize ------- with the minimum standards required for occupational safety.
(A) they
(B) theirs
(C) their
(D) themselves

122. Any questions ------- this month's assignments should be directed to Mr. Shaffer.
(A) up on
(B) according to
(C) related to
(D) through

123. At the current rates of production, Astra Industries will manufacture enough products to ------- expected demand by this summer.
(A) find
(B) meet
(C) enroll
(D) contact

124. Roster Industries and Charleston Co. are rumored to be ------- to completing their merger.
(A) closeness
(B) closing
(C) closely
(D) close

125. Equipment checked out from the media center must be returned ------- two weeks of the date it was borrowed.
(A) by
(B) within
(C) at
(D) before

126. Jackson Innovations discontinued one of their products, The Stomper, ------- due to safety concerns.
(A) reporting
(B) reports
(C) reported
(D) reportedly

127. The new Exgenera smart phone will not come out this month, ------- even next month, as the company is facing major design issues right now.
(A) whether
(B) by
(C) through
(D) or

128. Throughout his tenure, Mr. Spears has shown a great ------- to our university for the last three decades.
(A) collaboration
(B) resignation
(C) assurance
(D) commitment

129. Disappointed with the results of an internal audit, the president of Slantron Ltd. ------- reorganized the accounting and compliance departments.
(A) prompt
(B) promptly
(C) promptness
(D) prompter

130. At first, Dr. Sampson ------- the result of his experiment to a faulty machine, but he recently had the same result with new equipment.
(A) attributes
(B) attributed
(C) attributing
(D) attribution

Directions: Read the texts that follow. A word, phrase, or sentence is missing in parts of each text. Four answer choices are given below each of the texts. Select the best answer to complete the text. Then mark the letter (A), (B), (C), or (D) on your answer sheet.

Questions 131-134 refer to the following advertisement.

SPECIAL OFFER FROM OAKWOOD SPORTING GOODS

It's here—our end-of-season camping equipment sales event! As a previous customer of Jericho Sporting Goods, you ------- **131.** for a special offer not available to the public. We are offering 25 percent off on all camping and outdoor -------. **132.**

No down payment required! -------, customers who apply for **133.** in-house financing during this sales event can receive twelve months of no-interest payments.

-------. This offer expires December 15. **134.**

131. (A) qualifies
(B) to qualify
(C) qualify
(D) qualified

132. (A) gears
(B) geared
(C) gearing
(D) gear

133. (A) In addition
(B) As a result
(C) In contrast
(D) Even though

134. (A) A payment on your Oakwood Sporting Goods credit card is due
(B) Your account has recently been suspended
(C) We encourage you to visit us during the sales event
(D) Your first payment is due the end of November

GO ON TO THE NEXT PAGE.

PITTSBURGH — Shelton's Steak House, a new restaurant ------- 135.

in the Riverside neighborhood, will open for business on May 3.

The restaurant will offer a meat-lovers menu that emphasizes

------- ingredients. Shelton's specializes in steaks from Certified
136.

Angus beef, and American Yorkshire pork chops, flame-grilled

over mesquite charcoal. The restaurant will be open for lunch

Monday through Sunday from 11 A.M. to 3 P.M. and for dinner

from 5 P.M. until 10 P.M. -------. "Those looking for a great
137.

steak or chop are invited to stop by our restaurant." said owner

Gordon Shelton. "We welcome the opportunity to ------- both
138.

area residents and tourists."

135. (A) will locate
(B) locates
(C) located
(D) is located

136. (A) used
(B) separate
(C) sweet
(D) quality

137. (A) The restaurant might reopen in a different part of town
(B) These hours are similar to those of nearby eateries
(C) Customers have already provided some online reviews
(D) The restaurant has a simple, deep sea decor

138. (A) thank
(B) serve
(C) visit
(D) preserve

To: staff@melvoinindustries.com

From: d_timmons@melvoinindustries.com

Date: June 22

Subject: Zero Waste box

I am ------- to announce that our office has enrolled in an E-Waste
139.
recycling program through a company called Zero Waste. You
may have already noticed the Zero cardboard box next to the
printer. -------. Zero Waste sent this box to us to collect our used
140.
and unwanted electronic gadgets. Once the box is -------, I will
141.
ship it to the Zero Waste recycling facility, and we will be sent a
new one. Be sure to put only electronic waste in the box. The
company does not accept other -------. Thank you all for helping
142.
in our efforts to keep harmful metals and chemicals out of our
landfills.

Best,

Dan Timmons

Office Manager, Melvoin Industries

139. (A) pleasing
(B) pleasure
(C) please
(D) pleased

140. (A) It arrived a few days ago
(B) Let me know if it still works
(C) Just press the power button
(D) Take as many as you like

141. (A) found
(B) broken
(C) full
(D) clean

142. (A) ideas
(B) materials
(C) payments
(D) visitors

GO ON TO THE NEXT PAGE.

October 3

Terry Blankenship
80 West 34th Avenue
Kansas City, MO 64899

Dear Mr. Blankenship,

On behalf of the National Karate Museum, I want to thank you for your gift of $10,000. We are largely reliant on ------- like yours
143.
to maintain the quality of our exhibitions and related events. We appreciate your willingness to help us continue to grow and to make our museum ------- to as many people as possible.
144.

As one of our valued donors, you ------- to our Annual Supporters
145.
Gala later this year. -------. If you are in Colorado Springs at that
146.
time, we certainly hope to see you there.

Sincerely,
D. Q. Finley
Development Coordinator, National Karate Museum

143. (A) moments
(B) assistants
(C) contributions
(D) recommendations

144. (A) accessibly
(B) accessible
(C) accessed
(D) accessibility

145. (A) will be invited
(B) would have invited
(C) will invite
(D) would have been invited

146. (A) We have been in Colorado Springs for over twenty years
(B) Your keynote address was particularly inspiring
(C) The museum is open six days a week all year long
(D) More details about this event will be available soon

Directions: In this part you will read a selection of texts, such as magazine and newspaper articles, e-mails, and instant messages. Each text or set of texts is followed by several questions. Select the best answer for each question and mark the letter (A), (B), (C), or (D) on your answer sheet.

Questions 147-148 refer to the following Web page.

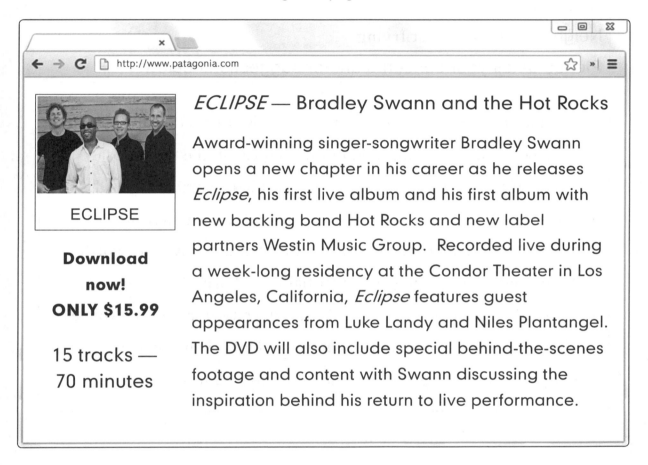

http://www.patagonia.com

ECLIPSE

Download now!
ONLY $15.99

15 tracks —
70 minutes

ECLIPSE — Bradley Swann and the Hot Rocks

Award-winning singer-songwriter Bradley Swann opens a new chapter in his career as he releases *Eclipse*, his first live album and his first album with new backing band Hot Rocks and new label partners Westin Music Group. Recorded live during a week-long residency at the Condor Theater in Los Angeles, California, *Eclipse* features guest appearances from Luke Landy and Niles Plantangel. The DVD will also include special behind-the-scenes footage and content with Swann discussing the inspiration behind his return to live performance.

147. What is indicated about *Eclipse*?
- (A) It was recorded during a series of live performances.
- (B) It will be released next year.
- (C) It is only available in one format.
- (D) It consists entirely of new songs.

148. What is stated about Bradley Swann?
- (A) He has played with musicians from different countries.
- (B) He has won awards for his music.
- (C) He retired from the music business nearly a decade ago.
- (D) He lives in Memphis, Tennessee.

GO ON TO THE NEXT PAGE.

CITY OF BROOMFIELD RESIDENT FEEDBACK FORM			
Name:	Ted Sippy	Phone:	(708)323-3459
Address:	9008 Belmont Avenue		
Neighborhood:	West Irving		
Please detail your concerns and/or suggestions below:			

Ever since construction began on Historic Route 66 (State Rte. 180), traffic has been very congested in the vicinity of the Ponderosa Parkway interchange (Interstate 40). Traffic is particularly bad during rush hours. As a result, many drivers are attempting to detour around this problem area by using Belmont Avenue, which cuts through West Irving, a residential neighborhood. In my opinion, this practice must stop. I urge the city to re-route vehicles without passing through our community. Only then can West Irving return to being the peaceful and safe area it once was.

149. Why did Mr. Sippy fill out the form?
(A) To support an upcoming construction project.
(B) To contest the removal of traffic signals.
(C) To protest an increase in local traffic.
(D) To criticize a historic tour.

150. What is suggested about Belmont Avenue?
(A) It was usually quiet.
(B) It crosses Ponderosa Parkway.
(C) It is under construction.
(D) It has several fast-food restaurants along it.

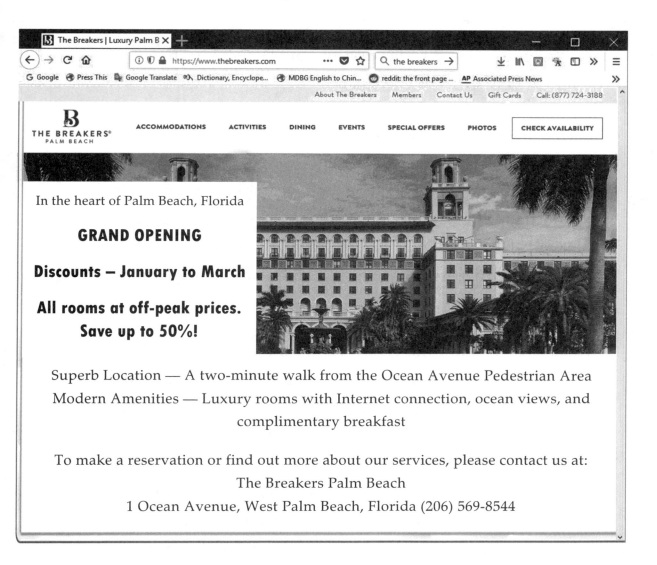

151. What is the purpose of this advertisement?
- (A) To announce a business seminar.
- (B) To advertise a museum opening.
- (C) To notify customers about a renovation of a gym.
- (D) To promote a new hotel.

152. What is NOT one of the attractive features offered?
- (A) Internet connection.
- (B) A complimentary meal.
- (C) A fitness center.
- (D) Ocean views.

GO ON TO THE NEXT PAGE.

To: All Spectra Branding Supervisors and Design Interns
From: Jill Boursten, Office Manager
Date: Friday, October 5
Subject: In-house software workshop

The in-house software workshop for new graphic design interns scheduled for Monday, October 8, at 9:00 a.m. has been postponed. This workshop is designed to familiarize interns with the software used by the creative department to format and develop all Spectra branding efforts.

Mason Reeves, the senior creative associate who developed the software, is unavailable on Monday. He has been asked to make an appearance at the CORE Marketing Summit in New York on both Monday and Tuesday. The workshop will therefore be rescheduled for Friday, October 12, at 10:00 a.m. Interns who are unable to attend this session are asked to notify their supervisors as soon as possible. Creative department supervisors, please ensure that all interns within your department are aware of the change by the end of the day today.

Thank you,
Jill

153. What is the memo about?
(A) A schedule change.
(B) A software update.
(C) A hiring policy.
(D) A company outing.

154. According to the memo, on what day will a workshop take place?
(A) Monday.
(B) Tuesday.
(C) Thursday.
(D) Friday.

Questions 155-157 refer to the following e-mail.

From:	a.abdul@javaplanet.com
To:	gil.manning@houstonorganicherald.com
Re:	Jave Planet
Date:	July 27

@ Java Beans Itinerary (2.67MB)

Dear Mr. Manning,

Everybody at Java Planet loves your popular website, which is an excellent resource for green-minded consumers in Houston. Since your site contains a list of related events in the area, I am writing to inform you of upcoming promotional activities for Earth Planet. I hope you will share this information with your readers.

Earth Planet has produced organic whole roasted coffee since our founding more than a decade ago, and we have just launched a unique blend of two exotic varieties from Sumatra and Bolivia. To advertise this line, Earth Planet will be distributing free samples at coffee shops, supermarkets, and health-food specialty outlets for the next few months. For your reference, I have attached the locations and dates of our marketing tour.

Should you have any questions or require additional information, feel free to contact me or visit our website, www.javaplanet.com. Furthermore, if you would like to try some of our products, please send your address, and I will be happy to oblige.

Sincerely,
Aliya Abdul
Vice President, Java Planet

155. What does Ms. Abdul ask Mr. Manning to do?
(A) Publicize some events.
(B) Attend a grand opening.
(C) Sponsor a marketing tour.
(D) Make an online donation.

156. What does Ms. Abdul offer to send?
(A) Order forms.
(B) Coffee samples.
(C) A press release.
(D) An offer of employment.

157. What is indicated about Java Planet?
(A) It recently opened a café in Houston.
(B) It owns a number of health-food stores.
(C) It has expanded its line of products.
(D) It will be launching a new website.

GO ON TO THE NEXT PAGE.

BUSINESS

☽ **30°**

FORECAST | TRAFFIC

| Weekly ads | Home | Local | Sports | Business | Opinion | Variety | Obituaries | Classifieds | Autos | Housing | Jobs |

Lighthizer to Expand This Summer

(NEW HAVEN) – According to a statement issued on Monday, Lighthizer's Brewery, headquartered in New Haven, has purchased the former Stamford Lumber Warehouse in Bridgeport. The 172-year-old brewery had hinted earlier this year that it planned to extend its market into Long Island and New York. Renovations to the 30,000-square-meter site are expected to begin in July, with the plant ready for operations in December.

Lighthizer's began as a small family-owned brewery in New Haven. Over the years, it has grown and opened breweries throughout Connecticut, including two in Stamford and three in Hartford. Lighthizer's now earns revenues of more than 300 million each year and has become one of the largest breweries on the East Coast.

In the past, Lighthizer's produced mainly Pilsner and Lager style beers. It also developed a reputation for its unique Uncle Bill's Pale Ale. Recently, however, the company has branched out into the specialty market, producing a variety of hand-made craft brews. It is not yet known if the Bridgeport plant will produce any new products.

158. What is the purpose of the article?
(A) To support an upcoming business merger.
(B) To announce the completion of a renovation project.
(C) To review a new product line.
(D) To report on a company's expansion.

159. What new items have recently been added to Lighthizer's product line?
(A) Pilsners.
(B) Lagers.
(C) Pale Ales.
(D) Craft beers.

160. Which Lighthizer's Brewery location is currently NOT producing any products?
(A) New Haven.
(B) Bridgeport.
(C) Stamford.
(D) Hartford.

SANTA BARBARA WINE COUNTRY
Only an hour from L.A.!

Spring is the perfect time for a visit to Santa Barbara Wine Country. Escape the crowded city streets for some relaxation.

Below is a sampling of what Santa Barbara has to offer at this beautiful time of year.

Wine Tastings — Delight your palette with Santa Barbara's only Master Sommelier, Rene Duchance, head winemaker at Cortesa Valley Vineyards. For the spring season, Mr. Duchance has chosen an especially inviting theme: Twenty Vineyards, Twenty Varietals. Purchase your tickets now at cortesavalley.com/20-20.

Mission Tours — Enjoy the breathtaking views of Santa Barbara Lake from the area's most famous Spanish mission, San Pancho. Tours run Tuesday through Sunday starting in May. There is no charge for tours, but they must be booked in advance.

Horseback Rides — Take advantage of the rustic terrain with an adventurous horseback ride on Santa Barbara Trail. Fares increase in the summer, and so do the tourists, so book your ride for early in the season. Horseback rides are available several times every day.

Hiking and Biking — The Santa Barbara National Park's many hiking trails can accommodate hikers of all levels. New color-coded maps have been posted throughout the park for your convenience, and bicycles are now permitted on certain paths! Before bicycling, be sure to read all guidelines for riding in the park, available on the Santa Barbara National Park page of our website.

Shakespeare on the Lawn — All plays are performed by local actors and theater students. Our season begins on April 7, with shows every Saturday and Sunday at 2:00 p.m. Children under five are free. Performances take place only if weather permits. Refunds are offered in case of inclement weather.

For more information, please go to: sbwinecountry.com

161. What is being advertised?
    (A) Events to celebrate Santa Barbara's anniversary.
    (B) Seasonal activities at a tourist destination.
    (C) A contest to win a vacation package.
    (D) Tours of a newly renovated area.

162. What is indicated about the plays?
    (A) They are performed in April only.
    (B) They are canceled when it rains.
    (C) They feature famous actors.
    (D) They receive excellent reviews.

163. According to the advertisement, why should people visit the Santa Barbara Wine Country page?
    (A) To book a tour of San Pancho Mission.
    (B) To rent a bicycle for riding on the park trails.
    (C) To learn about the rules for biking in the park.
    (D) To purchase tickets for guided tours of the park.

GO ON TO THE NEXT PAGE.

MEMORANDUM

ATTENTION:

All Johnson University graduate students residing in Hyde Park Dormitory

Date: August 24

We have been informed that the West Kennedy exit on the Fuller Expressway will be closed for repairs during the month of September between 8:00 a.m. and 5:00 p.m., Mondays through Saturdays. West Kennedy traffic will be redirected to the Hyde Park exit. If you are accustomed to using the West Kennedy exit to travel to the Silverstein Conservatory, please leave for classes early so you can still arrive on campus on schedule.

In response to the inconvenience, Dr. Virgil has offered to take extra passengers in his minivan each day. If you are interested in carpooling, please contact him directly. Dr. Virgil can accommodate five passengers on a first-come-first-served basis and asks $3.00 per day as compensation.

---

164. What is the memo mainly about?
(A) A change in a school schedule.
(B) The relocation of a bus stop.
(C) The impact of road construction.
(D) An application to live in a dormitory.

165. What is indicated about Dr. Virgil?
(A) He lives in West Kennedy.
(B) He starts work at 8:00 a.m.
(C) He can take some students to the university.
(D) He works at a hospital.

166. What are students encouraged to do?
(A) Reschedule their classes.
(B) Use public transportation.
(C) Attend a staff meeting.
(D) Allow extra time for travel.

167. The word "compensation" in paragraph 2, line 4, is closest in meaning to
(A) fuel.
(B) payment.
(C) correction.
(D) selection.

FOR IMMEDIATE RELEASE
Charles to Deliver Keynote at Meet_QLoc

LAS VEGAS (January 10) – Holden D. Charles, President of DMZ Computer Services, will deliver the keynote address at the Meet_QLoc User's Group Meeting to be held on February 20 at 9:00 a.m. in the Fulbright Ballroom of the Starwood Hotel in Las Vegas, Nevada.

Charles's talk, entitled "Multimedia Databases," will focus on methods to integrate images, sounds, and videos into QLoc databases. The registration fee is $125 for the entire day and includes lunch. Pre-registration is required due to seating limitations.

DMZ specializes in providing database solutions using QLoc. For more information on Charles's talk, contact Jane Qunnepac at (202) 445-1230. To register for the meeting, call the Washington-area QLoc Users' Group at (202) 445-8899.

168. What is the main purpose of the press release?
(A) To announce a business seminar.
(B) To promote a new project.
(C) To clarify the details of a merger.
(D) To request feedback from the public.

169. What will Mr. Charles most likely do on February 20?
(A) Sign a contract.
(B) Give a speech.
(C) Travel overseas.
(D) Take a new position.

170. What is included in the $125 registration fee?
(A) Parking.
(B) Transportation.
(C) A meal.
(D) A souvenir.

171. What is stated about DMZ Technologies?
(A) They specialize in databases.
(B) They are hosting the seminar.
(C) They are merging with another company.
(D) They are seeking new investors.

GO ON TO THE NEXT PAGE.

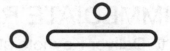

Florence Pineda   10:25 AM
John, has order JP-7326 been sent out yet? If not, the customer
has asked us to add item JD-6455A.

John D'Angelo   10:28 AM
That's a customized leather jacket, right? The embroidery
department usually requires a minimum of three days to
personalize an item.

Florence Pineda   10:29 AM
Can you get it any sooner? The customer needs it as soon as
possible.

John D'Angelo   10:31 AM
Let me check with someone from embroidery.

John D'Angelo   10:33 AM
Dawn, can you do a rush job on a jacket? It's item JD-6455A
for order number JP-7326.

Dawn Foster   10:34 AM
How soon do you need it? Is tomorrow OK?

Florence Pineda   10:35 AM
Yes, <u>that will have to do</u>. Thank you both for your help!

172. What type of products does the store sell?
- (A) Musical instruments.
- (B) Jewelry.
- (C) Clothing.
- (D) Appliances.

173. Why does Mr. D'Angelo contact Ms. Foster?
- (A) To find out when a meeting will be held.
- (B) To alert her to an error in a previous message.
- (C) To ask if some work can be completed faster than usual.
- (D) To find out when an order will be shipped.

174. What does the customer want to do?
- (A) Change an order.
- (B) Update a delivery address.
- (C) Receive a refund.
- (D) Choose a different shipping method.

175. At 10:35, what does Ms. Pineda most likely mean when she writes, "that will have to do"?
- (A) She plans to interview someone for a job.
- (B) She is satisfied with Ms. Foster's response.
- (C) The customer will be upset if the job can't be completed.
- (D) Some new items will be chosen for a catalog by the end of the day.

GO ON TO THE NEXT PAGE.

From the desk of

RICHARD & LOIS WEBBER

500 West Main Street
Middletown, DE 19709
(852) 343-1243

Mr. Lee Boatman
American Freight and Furniture Company
1920 Watterson Trail
Louisville, KY 40299

Dear Mr. Boatman,

We received our bed frame two weeks ago and are very happy. We love the finish and the quality and it looks great in our bedroom. We would like to know whether a matching set of night stands could be built. We looked through your catalog and liked the Mason Style shown on page 35. It matches our bed frame but would be too large for the limited amount of space we have. There is approximately two feet of clearance on either side of the bed. The Mason is 24" wide; we would need something closer to 18" wide.

If this is at all possible, please let us know. Thank you very much.

Richard & Lois Webber

FAX

TO: D.W. McCall   Number: 502-355-6096
FROM: Lee Boatman   Number: 502-223-2396

☐ Urgent   ☐ For review   ☐ Please comment   ☒ Please reply

Dear D.W.,

I hope all is well in Cleveland. I just received a request from a family for a pair of custom night stands. They already have a bed frame in the Mason Style (on page 25 in our catalog) and would like smaller versions of the matching night stands (page 35).

Please let me know if you have sufficient time and materials to <u>fulfill</u> this order, and I will send their specific size requirements. I wanted to check with you first since I know your woodwork is in high demand.

Thanks in advance.

Lee
americanfreight.us
+1 502-223-2396

---

176. What are Mr. and Ms. Webber requesting from Mr. Boatman?
(A) Pre-assembled toys.
(B) Custom furniture.
(C) Out of print books.
(D) Used records.

177. What is true about Mr. and Mrs. Webber?
(A) They are living in a one-room apartment.
(B) They are satisfied with their purchase.
(C) They are concerned about the price.
(D) They will order an item from a catalog.

178. Where do Mr. and Mrs. Webber live?
(A) Louisville.
(B) Middletown.
(C) Lexington.
(D) Paducah.

179. What is NOT suggested about Mr. McCall?
(A) He is busy in his job.
(B) He may not have the necessary materials.
(C) He has agreed to Mr. Boatman's request.
(D) He has worked with Mr. Boatman before.

180. In the fax, the word "fulfill" in paragraph 2, line 1 is closest in meaning to
(A) complete.
(B) appoint.
(C) refer.
(D) search.

GO ON TO THE NEXT PAGE.

From:	Noah Grist, Grist Produce
To:	Carly Deal, Sunny Valley Foods
Re:	Order GP0711-98 PARTIAL SHIPMENT
Date:	September 6

Carly,

As always, thank you very much for your business. I have sent via overnight express four cases of Haas avocados to your store in Valley, MO. Unfortunately, we could not send all ten cases of avocados you requested since they have sold out. Yours is the last shipment this season from our warehouse in Modesto, CA.

This is the fastest that we have ever sold out of any produce. This is most likely due to a recent article published in Harvester Magazine in which our Table Rock Merced Orchard was featured among California's most successful orchards. Since then, we have had an unprecedented number of orders. We are grateful for the attention, though we wish that we could better meet the demand.

If you are still interested in receiving the remaining six cases of avocados, please let me know. A friend of mine, Paul Shaffer, owns a small operation called Pilot Orchard in Visalia and I could possibly get you the remaining fruit.

Thank you for your continued patronage and best wishes to you.

N. Grist
Grist Produce, Director of Operations

Hey Paul,

How's everything at Pilot Orchard? Listen, I have just sold the last of my avocados and I still have several orders to fill. I'm guessing this has been busy season for you, too, but I was wondering if you have any remaining avocados that I can buy. If so, they can be sent to me at my warehouse. I will call you later today to discuss the payment and other details.

Are you planning on attending next month's California Growers' Association meeting? It has been a while since we've had a meeting and it will be nice to see how everyone is doing.

I look forward to talking to you soon.

GO ON TO THE NEXT PAGE. ➔

181. What does the first e-mail indicate about Ms. Deal?
    (A) She has ordered from Grist Produce before.
    (B) She works in California.
    (C) She writes for Harvester Magazine.
    (D) She owns an orchard.

182. According to the first e-mail, what has affected the number of orders received by Grist Produce?
    (A) A change in shipping methods.
    (B) Production of avocados at nearby farms.
    (C) Publicity provided by a magazine.
    (D) A decrease in competition in the region.

183. What does Mr. Grist offer to do for Ms. Deal?
    (A) Check whether another grower has avocados.
    (B) Issue a full refund.
    (C) Include her company in a magazine article.
    (D) Fill the remaining order with a different item.

184. Where would Mr. Shaffer and Pilot Orchard send the order of avocados?
    (A) To Visalia.
    (B) To Valley.
    (C) To Modesto.
    (D) To Table Rock Merced.

185. How will Mr. Grist and Mr. Shaffer discuss the price of avocados?
    (A) In person.
    (B) Over the phone.
    (C) At a meeting.
    (D) By fax.

Questions 186-190 refer to the following article, schedule, and e-mail.

FINANCIAL GURU ON TOUR

New York (July 7) — Martha Leonard, one of America's most prominent financial advisors and owner of a financial services company for the past 20 years, will be giving a series of talks on various financial topics beginning one week from today.

On July 14, Ms. Leonard will speak at New York's Central Library. On July 15 and 16, she will speak at Chicago's McCormick Place Convention Center. On July 17, she will speak at Houston's City Conference Center. On July 18, she will speak at Denver's Memorial Library, and finally on 19 July, she will head to San Jose to give a talk at the McEnery Auditorium.

Tickets are limited. Visit www.leonardfinancial.com for prices and other information.

Martha Leonard's July Speaking Tour Schedule

City	Topic	Date	Time
New York	Mutual Funds – Emerging Trends & Funds	July 14	7:00
Chicago	Commodity Cycles in Emerging Markets	July 15	8:00
Chicago	Pension Maximization Using Life Insurance	July 16	7:30
Houston	Investing in Today's Economy	July 17	7:00
Denver	Commodity Cycles in Emerging Markets	July 18	7:30
San Jose	Traditional Cash Reserves	July 19	7:00

From:	j.lillard@leonardfinacial.com
To:	a.miller@technet.com
Re:	Martha Leonard Speaking Tour
Date:	July 10

Dear Mr. Miller,

Thank you for your interest in Ms. Leonard's speaking tour. Unfortunately, the event you inquired about in Denver has already sold out. However, Ms. Leonard will be giving the same talk in Chicago on July 15, and that event presently has seats available.

Alternatively, if you would like to set up an appointment with Ms. Leonard to discuss her services directly via phone or videoconference, I would be happy to arrange that for you.

Regards,

Jasmine Lillard
Leonard Financial

186. What is indicated about Ms. Leonard?
(A) She lives in Houston.
(B) She gives free talks at libraries.
(C) She tours Europe every summer.
(D) She has operated a business for 20 years.

187. Where will the talk regarding cash reserves be given?
(A) At the Memorial Library.
(B) At the City Conference Center.
(C) At the McCormick Place Convention Center.
(D) At the McEnery Auditorium.

188. What is the purpose of the e-mail?
(A) To arrange a speaking engagement.
(B) To decline an offer.
(C) To respond to a question.
(D) To confirm a change to a schedule.

189. What event date was Mr. Miller originally interested in?
(A) July 16.
(B) July 17.
(C) July 18.
(D) July 19.

190. What most likely is Ms. Lillard's job?
(A) Graphic designer.
(B) Administrative assistant.
(C) Journalist.
(D) Ticket agent.

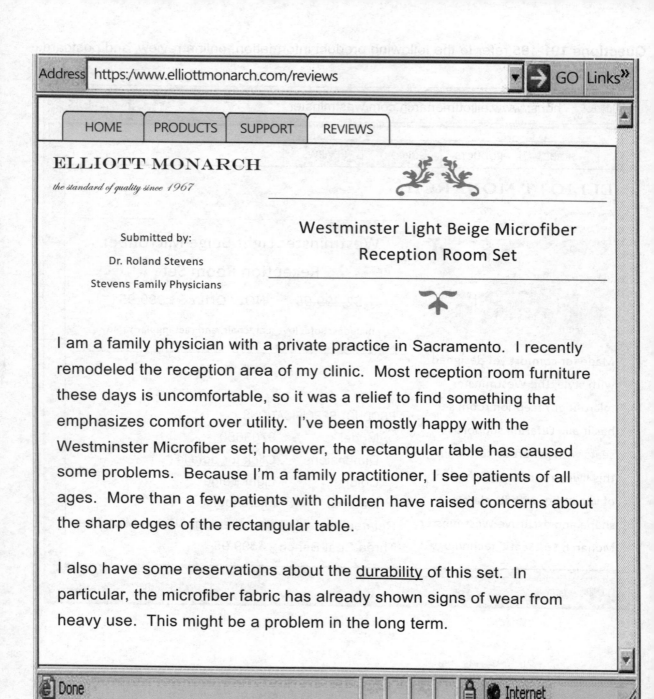

Address https:/www.elliottmonarch.com/reviews   ▼ → GO Links»

| HOME | PRODUCTS | SUPPORT | REVIEWS |

ELLIOTT MONARCH
the standard of quality since 1967

Submitted by:

Dr. Roland Stevens

Stevens Family Physicians

Westminster Light Beige Microfiber Reception Room Set

I am a family physician with a private practice in Sacramento. I recently remodeled the reception area of my clinic. Most reception room furniture these days is uncomfortable, so it was a relief to find something that emphasizes comfort over utility. I've been mostly happy with the Westminster Microfiber set; however, the rectangular table has caused some problems. Because I'm a family practitioner, I see patients of all ages. More than a few patients with children have raised concerns about the sharp edges of the rectangular table.

I also have some reservations about the <u>durability</u> of this set. In particular, the microfiber fabric has already shown signs of wear from heavy use. This might be a problem in the long term.

Done   🔒 🌐 Internet

ELLIOTT MONARCH

the standard of quality since 1967

151 BURLINGTON AVENUE, PALO ALTO, CA 94322

(415)834-0009

Dear Dr. Stevens,

We're sorry to hear about your trouble with our product. As a result of feedback like yours, we've introduced a new rectangular table with softer edges. If you contact us at: **customersupport@elliottmonarch.com**, we'll send you, in Light Beige, a duplicate of the table to complement your Westminster set. Note that this gift will be sent to you after you verify that you posted the online review.

We also hear your concerns about our microfiber technology. Rest assured that our lightweight fabric has been proven to withstand years' worth of rough treatment, maintaining its integrity after over 100,000 uses tested under stressful conditions in our laboratories.

Irene Coo, Elliott Monarch customer service

191. What does Dr. Stevens write about his furniture?
(A) He likes the color.
(B) The cushions are too soft.
(C) He purchased the set recently.
(D) The table injures his patients.

192. In the review, the word "durability" in paragraph 2, line 1, is closest in meaning to
(A) strength.
(B) force.
(C) size.
(D) intelligence.

193. What does Ms. Coo offer to Dr. Stevens?
(A) A full set of reception room furniture.
(B) A new sofa.
(C) A new loveseat.
(D) A new table.

194. What must Dr. Stevens do in order to receive a gift from Elliott Monarch?
(A) Retract negative feedback given on a website.
(B) Send a copy of his purchase order.
(C) Prove that he is the author of a product review.
(D) Complete a survey about new products.

195. What does Ms. Coo indicate about the table?
(A) It has been discontinued.
(B) It has been redesigned.
(C) It is out of stock.
(D) It is on sale.

GO ON TO THE NEXT PAGE.

Drexel Institute of Technology

Intermediate Craft Beer Brewing Course
CB-0002
Instructor: Joe Long

Cost: $150

This six-week course is designed to take the students on a journey through the world of craft beer. Each class will tap into a different area of craft beer. Some of the topics we will cover include the history of beer, the craft beer revolution, beer styles, beer and food pairings and many more. This course will serve as a general overview of craft beer and its role in today's culture. Intermediate Craft Beer will give you the foundation for all future courses in the program. If you don't already appreciate craft beer, you will when you have completed this course!

This course will expand on the introduction to brewing that is covered in CB 0001. Students will gain a deeper understanding of brewing terminology, as well as how the manipulation of raw ingredients and brewing practices result in the wide variety of beer styles. Our goal is to give students a stronger <u>foundation</u> in the art and science of brewing, so that they may serve the needs of the industry in a more thorough and insightful manner. The course will include a field trip to a local brewery. All course ingredients will be provided.

CB 0002 Course Description

Week 1 – Saturday, April 4, 9:00 a.m.

Short overview of grain brewing

The 12 myths of brewing dispelled

The 7 secrets to making good beer

Week 2 – Sat., April 11, 9:00 a.m.

All about Malt

Malting and Adjuncts

All about Hops

Week 3 – Sat., April 18, 9:00 a.m.

Yeast and Fermentation

Mashing

Designing a Beer

Week 4 – Sat., April 25, 8:00 a.m.

(Please note earlier start time)

Brew Day at Brady Brewery

Lunch

Week 5 – Sat., May 2, 9:00 a.m.

Hygiene, bottling, kegging and filtration

Home filtration

Water, oxygen pick up, oxygen ingress

Week 6 – Sat., May 16, 10:00 a.m.

(Please note later start time)

Final exam

Further Note: Additional brewing time at Drexel Institute is available on Sundays from 9:00 a.m. to 5:00 p.m. for those who would like more time with an instructor present. If you are interested in time with an instructor outside these hours, we recommend that you call ahead or be prepared to work independently.

GO ON TO THE NEXT PAGE.

WHILE YOU WERE OUT	
NAME:	Joe Long
DATE/TIME:	March 30, 3:05 PM

~~Telephone~~	Fax	Email	Office Visit

MESSAGE:	Devin Yates called. He is taking CB 0002. He has a scheduling issue with the Brew Day trip and wondered if it would be OK for him to skip it. I told him that you would call him back to discuss it further. Please reach him at 595-8129.
TAKEN BY:	Norm Smith

196. What is suggested about the brewing course?
(A) It will expand on a previous course.
(B) All ingredients must be purchased from the school.
(C) Students are required to be at least 18 years of age.
(D) It lasts five weeks.

197. What does the course description indicate?
(A) Drexel Institute recently expanded its parking lot.
(B) Instructors may reschedule a regular class to meet on Sunday.
(C) Administrators invite suggestions for new classes.
(D) Instructors can provide assistance outside of class time.

198. In the brochure, the word "foundation" in paragraph 2, line 5, is the closest in meaning to
(A) shelter.
(B) guarantee.
(C) material.
(D) basis.

199. What is most likely true about Mr. Yates?
(A) He is under 18 years of age.
(B) He works at Brady Brewery.
(C) He is a master brewer.
(D) He has taken a previous course.

200. To which class session does the phone message most likely refer?
(A) Week 2.
(B) Week 3.
(C) Week 4.
(D) Week 5.

Stop! This is the end of the test. If you finish before time is called, you may go back to Parts 5, 6, and 7 and check your work.

New TOEIC Listening Script

PART 1

1. (   ) (A) Some people are in a bank.
   (B) Some people are in a lobby.
   (C) Some people are in a restaurant.
   (D) Some people are in an auditorium.

2. (   ) (A) The boys are seated to the left of the woman.
   (B) The boys are hugging to the right of the woman.
   (C) The boys are fighting in front of the woman.
   (D) The boys are laughing behind the woman.

3. (   ) (A) The car has a siren on its roof.
   (B) The truck has a crane mounted on the back.
   (C) The train has a section for smokers.
   (D) The bus has a rack for bicycles.

4. (   ) (A) Some people are swimming in a pond.
   (B) Some people are sitting in cubicles.
   (C) Some people are standing in line.
   (D) Some people are lying in bed.

5. (   ) (A) The woman is holding some books.
   (B) The woman is washing some clothes.
   (C) The woman is reading to some children.
   (D) The woman is working with some bricks.

6. (   ) (A) The man is painting a wall.
   (B) The man is replacing a light bulb.
   (C) The man is testing a smoke detector.
   (D) The man is grilling a steak.

GO ON TO THE NEXT PAGE.

PART 2

7. (　　) Who signed for the delivery?
   (A) Ms. Harris.
   (B) May 22th.
   (C) Seventy-five dollars.

8. (　　) Should I turn on the air conditioning?
   (A) The floor looks slippery.
   (B) Yes, it's hot in here.
   (C) With cream and sugar, please.

9. (　　) Where will your booth be at the farmer's market?
   (A) Near the north exit.
   (B) There's nothing left.
   (C) Before the growing season.

10. (　　) The office feels empty today.
   (A) Several staff members are absent.
   (B) No, I told her to come early.
   (C) The weekly weather forecast.

11. (　　) When did we last update our website?
   (A) Last week.
   (B) Yes, I read that this morning.
   (C) The paint isn't dry yet.

12. (　　) Who's appearing in our next cosmetics ad campaign?
   (A) They'll be shot on location.
   (B) A world-famous supermodel.
   (C) Here's a pen that works.

13. (　　) How did Mr. Finch react when his policy proposal was rejected?
   (A) Everyone except Rondell.
   (B) He was discouraged, of course.
   (C) In last week's financial forecast.

14. (　　) Do you want the morning or the afternoon flight to Tampa?
   (A) Let me check my schedule.
   (B) The café across the street.
   (C) Just once a week.

15. (   ) The Internet is working now, isn't it?
     (A) I like the logo, too.
     (B) I already had some.
     (C) No, I'm still having issues.

16. (   ) Can you take a look at the schedule for next week?
     (A) It's in a convenient location.
     (B) Sure, I'll do it in a minute.
     (C) By overnight delivery?

17. (   ) Why have they blocked off Taylor Street?
     (A) A water main burst.
     (B) Only two blocks.
     (C) No, I don't believe it's true.

18. (   ) Hasn't the delivery truck been loaded yet?
     (A) That option is best.
     (B) Sure, I'll download that program.
     (C) No, some items had to be repackaged.

19. (   ) Fiona Oliver was transferred to a different department, wasn't she?
     (A) The driver is on his way.
     (B) The appliances are all new.
     (C) Yes, she's in Marketing now.

20. (   ) How do I access the hotel's business center?
     (A) It's 25 dollars per day.
     (B) Use your hotel key card.
     (C) No, I don't think it does.

21. (   ) I'm thinking about attending the professional development seminar.
     (A) Take a left at the corner.
     (B) October 20th and 27th.
     (C) I personally found it very helpful.

22. (   ) Do you think it's OK to park my car here for now?
     (A) The sign says "By permit only."
     (B) That's a dangerous part of town.
     (C) Just three minutes.

GO ON TO THE NEXT PAGE.

23. (   ) Which restaurant are we taking our clients to this evening?
  (A) Sure, thanks!
  (B) I thought we had reservations at Tribeca Bistro.
  (C) Usually around 8 o'clock.

24. (   ) Where's the Kimball Theater?
  (A) There's a floor plan near the elevator.
  (B) I moved to a different room.
  (C) Lee's presentation is after mine.

25. (   ) Who do you recommend for legal services?
  (A) We can pay by credit card.
  (B) Their fees have nearly doubled.
  (C) I need to find someone as well.

26. (   ) When do you finish work today?
  (A) Well, I still have a lot to do.
  (B) Does Steve also work there?
  (C) He was in the conference room.

27. (   ) Are you serious about finding a new job?
  (A) Some computer consultants.
  (B) The monthly budget report.
  (C) Yeah, I'm done here.

28. (   ) Why did Ms. Wrightwood cancel the product launch?
  (A) Actually, she just pushed it back a week.
  (B) What time is our flight?
  (C) I'd like the next available opening.

29. (   ) Could you take the late shift for me tomorrow evening?
  (A) Just leave it here.
  (B) Yes, it is getting cold outside.
  (C) Sorry, I have tickets to the baseball game.

30. (   ) How much will it cost to send these packages?
  (A) About seven days.
  (B) This type of packaging, please.
  (C) When do you want them to arrive?

31. (   ) Have you printed out my itinerary?
  (A) I thought you wanted to reschedule two meetings.
  (B) Round trip tickets are expensive.
  (C) Helen is taking his place.

PART 3

Questions 32 through 34 *refer to the following conversation.*

M : Hello, this is Lieutenant Vance calling from the Riverside Police Department. I see here that you will be bringing your students to the station for a tour and first-aid demonstration. Do you have a final count of how many people, students and guardians, will be coming?

W : Yes, we'll be 32 people in total. I can email you a list of names later today.

M : Perfect! That way, we can print up some personalized visitor badges for each one of you.

32. (   ) Where does the man work?
  (A) At a police station.
  (B) At a school library.
  (C) At a transportation company.
  (D) At a theater.

33. (   ) What does the man ask about?
  (A) When a meeting will start.
  (B) Where a business is located.
  (C) How many visitors are expected.
  (D) How the bill will be paid.

34. (   ) What will the man prepare?
  (A) Informational brochures.
  (B) Name badges.
  (C) Training manuals.
  (D) An expense report.

Questions 35 through 37 *refer to the following conversation.*

W : This is Ashley Earl speaking.

M : Ms. Earl, this is Willie Spires from SkyHigh Airlines. I'm calling about your delayed baggage. It has finally arrived at the airport and I can have it sent to you this afternoon.

W : That's good to know, but I won't be home this afternoon. Could you possibly leave the suitcase by the front door of my house?

GO ON TO THE NEXT PAGE.

M : I'm afraid we need someone to sign for it so we can make sure it's been delivered.

W : Well, how about leaving it with my next door neighbor? He frequently signs for my deliveries. He's retired and home during the day. I can call him and let him know you're coming.

35. (   ) What is the purpose of the telephone call?
    (A) To arrange a delivery.
    (B) To request an upgrade.
    (C) To place an order.
    (D) To confirm a reservation.

36. (   ) What does the man say is required?
    (A) A passport.
    (B) A credit card.
    (C) A signature.
    (D) A security code.

37. (   ) Who does the woman say she will call?
    (A) Her lawyer.
    (B) Her boss.
    (C) Her husband.
    (D) Her neighbor.

Questions 38 through 40 *refer to the following conversation between three speakers.*

M : Excuse me, I had dinner in your restaurant last night and I think I may have left my credit card at the table.
Woman UK : Hmm... OK. Let me check with Rachel. She was the supervising manager on duty last night.

M : I'd appreciate it. I really hope the card didn't get thrown in the trash.
Woman UK : I doubt it... Oh, here she is. Hey, Rachel. A customer thinks he may have left his credit card at his table last night. Anything turn up?

Woman US : Oh, we did find a card last night. May I have your name, sir?
M : It's Phil Robertson, and the card is an Urbanbank Visa.

Woman US : That's it. I have it locked in the safe in the manager's office. I'll go get it.

38. (   ) Where are the speakers?
    (A) At a shoe store.
    (B) At a print shop.
    (C) At a dry cleaner.
    (D) At a restaurant.

39. (   ) Why is the man at the restaurant?
    (A) To return some equipment.
    (B) To pick up some samples.
    (C) To look for a missing item.
    (D) To discuss a catering order.

40. (   ) What does Rachel ask about?
    (A) A price.
    (B) A color.
    (C) A location.
    (D) A name.

Questions 41 through 43 *refer to the following conversation.*

M : Hi, this is Greg from Clearview Window and Door Company. We installed new window blinds in your house last month. I'm calling to find out if you're satisfied with the service you received.

W : Overall, I'm pleased with the service, but the blinds I ordered were originally out of stock. That caused a delay, but when the blinds became available, your guys did a great job.

M : I'm glad to hear you're satisfied with our service. And I see in my records that your original purchase included a 10 percent discount for first-time customers?

W : Um...not to my knowledge. I paid the full amount.

M : That was a mistake on our end. I'll process a 10 percent refund and send a check right away.

41. (   ) Why is the man calling?
    (A) To confirm payment information.
    (B) To request customer feedback.
    (C) To offer a free consultation.
    (D) To reschedule an installation.

42. (   ) What caused a delay?
    (A) An appointment was missed.
    (B) A product was temporarily unavailable.
    (C) Some equipment was faulty.
    (D) Some forms were misplaced.

43. (   ) What does the man say he will do?
    (A) Send some product samples.
    (B) Inspect some merchandise.
    (C) Pass on some information.
    (D) Issue a refund.

GO ON TO THE NEXT PAGE.

W : Hi, I just moved into the building and I'm interested in joining your fitness center. Could you give me a brief overview of the facility?

Man UK : Of course. We're open seven days a week, 24 hours a day. In addition to free classes, members have access to indoor basketball and tennis courts, exercise equipment, and a swimming pool.

W : Exactly what I'm looking for. Is there a discount for tenants of the building?

Man UK : Ah... I'm not sure. Joe, are we still offering the tenant discount?

Man US : Yes, as long as you can prove residency, you'll be eligible for a 50 percent discount on your first year of membership.

W : Umm... I just moved in, so I don't have anything except a copy of my lease. Will that work?

Man US : Sure.

W : Great! So I'd like to sign up today. Do I just need to fill out an application?

Man UK : Yes, I have one right here.

44. (　　) Where are the speakers?
    (A) At a university library.
    (B) At a train station.
    (C) At a fitness center.
    (D) At a sports stadium.

45. (　　) Why does the woman need to verify her residency?
    (A) To vote in an election.
    (B) To make a reservation.
    (C) To verify her date of birth.
    (D) To receive a discount.

46. (　　) What will the woman most likely do next?
    (A) Complete some paperwork.
    (B) Make an online payment.
    (C) Speak to a manager.
    (D) Sign a lease.

W : Though it took a long time to come up with the shape of this energy drink bottle, I think our clients will be happy with the design. It's very attractive.

M : I agree. Moreover, it's made entirely from recycled materials, which is just what the client requested.

W : Right. I'm pleased that everything is going so well.

M : Me too. Hey... a quick question. You know, I play on the company softball team, right? Well, we have a tournament starting on Friday. Would it be OK if I leave early that afternoon?

W : Well, we still have to work on the label for the bottle, but I think we can spare you for a couple of hours on Friday.

47. (　　) What are the speakers working on?
       (A) A bottle design.
       (B) A tax audit.
       (C) An advertising budget.
       (D) A training manual.

48. (　　) What does the man say about the company softball team?
       (A) The team is receiving an award.
       (B) The team is participating in a competition.
       (C) The players are male and female.
       (D) The players are getting new uniforms.

49. (　　) Why does the woman say, "I think we can spare you for a couple of hours on Friday"?
       (A) To extend an approaching deadline.
       (B) To disagree with a colleague's opinion.
       (C) To approve the man's request.
       (D) To express dissatisfaction with the client's request.

Questions 50 through 52 *refer to the following conversation.*

W : Thanks for meeting me in the café today, Kyle. I think it's nice to get out of the office every now and then. Plus, I like to meet with new employees in a more casual setting. So, how's everything going?

M : Everything is great, Maryanne. I'm just about to submit my first consumer survey report, and I'd appreciate your feedback. I had trouble finding enough customers willing to volunteer for the survey in order to get a wide enough range of responses.

W : Unfortunately, survey participants can be difficult to secure. Did you use our company's online database? It has a list of names of our recent customers. I find that new customers are the most willing to participate in surveys.

GO ON TO THE NEXT PAGE.

50. (　　) Why did the woman want to meet with the man?
   (A) To follow up on a job offer.
   (B) To congratulate the man on a nomination.
   (C) To return a favor.
   (D) To ask the man about his progress at work.

51. (　　) What does the man say he had trouble with?
   (A) Submitting a report.
   (B) Finding volunteers for a survey.
   (C) Formatting a website.
   (D) Receiving international shipments.

52. (　　) What does the woman suggest the man do?
   (A) Read a company handbook.
   (B) Participate in a training session.
   (C) Use a database.
   (D) Talk to a coordinator.

Questions 53 through 55 refer to the following conversation.

M : I've got good news, Betty. I was able to book Rolling Jams to perform at our club on April 17th.

W : That is good news! I love those guys. I'll add them to the musician schedule on the April poster.

M : Listen, about the poster. Thanks for doing it, by the way. Your design is perfect. But I'm just wondering about printing in black and white. Shouldn't we print in color?

W : We should, but color printing is going to be way more expensive.

M : Eh... I'll take a look at a budget and I'll let you know if we can afford it.

53. (　　) What is scheduled for April 17?
   (A) A board meeting.
   (B) A cooking demonstration.
   (C) A musical performance.
   (D) A fitness center reopening.

54. (　　) What does the man thank the woman for?
   (A) Creating a poster.
   (B) Revising a calendar.
   (C) Booking an artist.
   (D) Responding to a complaint.

55. (   ) What does the man say he will do?
  (A) Contact a print shop.
  (B) Listen to a recording.
  (C) Check a budget.
  (D) Update a schedule.

Questions 56 through 58 _refer to the following conversation._

M : Welcome back from the trade fair, Michelle. Did you get any orders for our countertop grills?

W : I met a lot of new customers at the show, but I have so many business cards to sort out. It always takes so long.

M : You should download an app for your phone to organize them. I just found one called Digital Rolodex. You take a picture of each card and the app converts all the text to digital format. Then you can easily search for what you need.

W : I could really use that. Is it free?

M : There is a free version, but the premium version lets you store an unlimited number of cards. It's well worth the price.

56. (   ) What has the woman recently done?
  (A) Led a product demonstration.
  (B) Attended a trade show.
  (C) Ordered business cards.
  (D) Submitted a proposal.

57. (   ) What does the man think the woman should do?
  (A) Write a review.
  (B) Buy a new camera.
  (C) Organize a party.
  (D) Use a phone application.

58. (   ) What does the man like about the premium version of a product?
  (A) It is easier to use.
  (B) It is the industry standard.
  (C) It has more storage space.
  (D) It comes with warranty.

Questions 59 through 61 _refer to the following conversation._

M : So, Ms. Binghampton, you believe that your lower back pain may be causing your headaches?

W : Well, I sit at a desk for 10 hours a day.

GO ON TO THE NEXT PAGE.

M : I suggest you get up and stretch every 30 minutes when seated for long periods of time. Take a five-minute stroll around the office. Just something to get your blood moving.

W : Do I need to see a chiropractor about the back pain?

M : Not right now. Let's try this first. If the headaches continue, we'll consider seeing a specialist.

59. (   ) Who most likely is the man?
    (A) A mechanic.
    (B) A lawyer.
    (C) A doctor.
    (D) A teacher.

60. (   ) Why does the woman say, "I sit at a desk for 10 hours a day"?
    (A) To request a second opinion.
    (B) To apologize for an error.
    (C) To describe her area of expertise.
    (D) To explain the cause of a problem.

61. (   ) What does the man recommend the woman do?
    (A) Rearrange her work space.
    (B) Put her name on a waiting list.
    (C) Join a fitness center.
    (D) Take breaks at certain intervals.

Questions 62 through 64 refer to the following conversation and brochure.

M : I just heard at the staff meeting that our IT department manager, Mr. Edwards, is relocating out of state. I think they'll want someone internal to take over.

W : I know. I'd be interested in being the next manager, but I'm a little nervous about applying. What if the hiring committee thinks I don't have a strong enough background in website administration?

M : Well, the local community center offers advanced computer classes. You should enroll in one.

W : That'd be great if there's one I could attend. I work from 8 a.m. to 6 p.m. weekdays. So, hopefully, there's a session in the evening or on the weekend.

M : They offer different sessions, so I'm sure you'd find one that fits your schedule.

62. (   ) What was announced at the staff meeting?
    (A) A sales event will be held.
    (B) An employee will leave the company.
    (C) A merger will take place.
    (D) A new product will be launched.

63. (　　) What is the woman nervous about doing?
  (A) Applying for a job.
  (B) Taking an exam.
  (C) Being interviewed for an article.
  (D) Starting her own company.

64. (　　) Look at the graphic. Which session will the woman most likely attend?
  (A) Session 1.
  (B) Session 2.
  (C) Session 3.
  (D) Session 4.

Radcliff Heights Community Center		
Advanced Computer Classes		
Session 1	Database Management	Mondays at 11:00 a.m.
Session 2	Network Security	Wednesdays at 5:30 p.m.
Session 3	Website Administration	Thursdays at 6:00 p.m.
Session 4	Website Administration	Saturdays at 1:00 p.m.

Questions 65 through 67 refer to the following conversation and menu.

W : I hope you enjoyed your fish and chips. Can I bring you anything for dessert? It's included since you ordered the daily special.

M : The fish and chips were delicious, thanks, but I don't want any dessert. Just a cup of coffee, black, please. But I do have a question, though. Does your restaurant do any catering?

W : Oh, certainly. I'll bring you our catering and takeout menu. Anything other than coffee I can get you?

M : Just the check, please. And I should mention that I have a coupon for 25 percent off my meal, so I'll be using that.

W : I'm sorry, but unfortunately, that coupon is valid for regular menu items only, not the daily specials.

65. (　　) Look at the graphic. What day is the conversation taking place?
  (A) Tuesday.
  (B) Wednesday.
  (C) Thursday.
  (D) Friday.

GO ON TO THE NEXT PAGE.

```
------------------------------------
        Nibbler's Oceanview Restaurant
               Daily Specials

                  Monday
               Catch of the Day

                  Tuesday
                Clam Chowder

                 Wednesday
                Fish and Chips

                  Thursday
        All You Can Eat Shrimp Buffet

                   Friday
             Surf and Turf Platter
        ------------------------------------
```

66. (   ) What does the man ask about?
    (A) Outdoor seating.
    (B) Group discounts.
    (C) Catering services.
    (D) Vegetarian options.

67. (   ) Why does the woman apologize?
    (A) She cannot accept a coupon.
    (B) She cannot issue a refund.
    (C) A meal course was not delivered.
    (D) An area is closed for remodeling.

Questions 68 through 70 *refer to the following conversation and chart.*

W : I'm looking forward to our business trip on Tuesday. But I wish we didn't have to deal with
    Santa Fe train station. They never have enough ticket agents on staff. At least we can get
    our tickets online instead.

M : Their website makes it easy to buy tickets. Now, we need to choose our seats. How about
    the first economy coach car?

W : Actually, I'll have some phone calls to make on the way and I can't do that in a coach.

M : OK, well, only one regular sleeper car has seats still available, so we should take that.

W : Do you want to use the company credit card for this?

M : No, I'll use my own card and get reimbursed later.

68. (   ) Why does the woman dislike Santa Fe train station?
    (A) It has no Internet access.
    (B) It is being renovated.
    (C) It is always understaffed.
    (D) It is inconveniently located.

69. (   ) Look at the graphic. Which car will the speakers most likely choose?
    (A) Car 1.
    (B) Car 2.
    (C) Car 3.
    (D) Car 4.

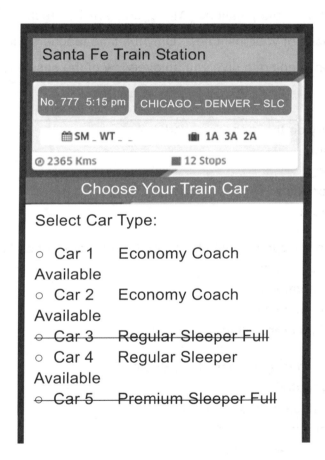

70. (   ) What does the woman ask the man about?
    (A) What time he wants to return.
    (B) Where he wants to meet.
    (C) How he wants to pay.
    (D) How much luggage he is bringing.

GO ON TO THE NEXT PAGE.

PART 4

Questions 71 through 73 _refer to the following excerpt from a meeting._

Obviously, we hold these manager meetings to secure and promote a consistent level of student satisfaction throughout our chain of language institutes. However, we've discovered that the quality of student experience varies from one location to the next. That's why I've hired Ms. Paulson here to develop monthly training sessions for full-time teachers at all of our locations. Managers, you'll be responsible for directing these sessions at each of your institutes. Only full-time teachers will be required to attend. Ms. Paulson is going to give you an overview of the sessions now. Let's welcome her.

71. (   ) What industry do the managers work in?
      (A) Education.
      (B) Marketing.
      (C) Transportation.
      (D) Restaurant.

72. (   ) According to the speaker, what area of the business needs to be improved?
      (A) Personnel retention.
      (B) Staff recruitment.
      (C) Customer service.
      (D) Curriculum preparation.

73. (   ) What will the managers most likely do next?
      (A) Meet new students.
      (B) Submit student grade reports.
      (C) Conduct a training session.
      (D) Listen to a presentation.

Questions 74 through 76 _refer to the following telephone message._

Hi, this is Charlotte Denier calling from Hacienda Hotel Group regarding your job application for the senior marketing position. Your resume is solid and we'd like to discuss this opportunity with you in person. But before we take the next step, I just want to remind you that the HHG marketing department has only recently been developed and is still in the development stage. Thus, your initial duties may vary from time to time until we are fully staffed. If this is something you're interested in, give me a call back to set up a time for an interview. My number is 875-2233. Have a nice day.

74. (   ) What type of company does the speaker work for?
    (A) An electronics manufacturer.
    (B) A travel agency.
    (C) A hotel chain.
    (D) An accounting firm.

75. (   ) What does the speaker mention about the position?
    (A) It requires official certification.
    (B) It is in a newly established department.
    (C) It involves frequent travel.
    (D) It is a part-time position.

76. (   ) Why is the listener asked to return a call?
    (A) To provide a reference.
    (B) To negotiate a salary.
    (C) To schedule an interview.
    (D) To confirm a delivery.

Questions 77 through 79 *refer to the following excerpt from a meeting.*

OK, I think that just about covers everything for this marketing meeting. Oh, one more item. I want to take a minute to tell you about our new line of women's accessories, but we'll have to schedule a separate session for that next week. Meanwhile, I'd like you to take a look at the specifications of the new fall fashion line. The catalog can be found on the company website. Please be prepared to share your advertising strategy ideas for these products at our next meeting.

77. (   ) What department do the listeners work in?
    (A) Maintenance.
    (B) Purchasing.
    (C) Information Technology.
    (D) Marketing.

GO ON TO THE NEXT PAGE.

78. (   ) What does the speaker say is available on a company website?
  (A) An employee directory.
  (B) A catalog.
  (C) A map.
  (D) A schedule.

79. (   ) What does the speaker ask the listeners to do at the next meeting?
  (A) Choose a logo.
  (B) Elect a representative.
  (C) Discuss their ideas.
  (D) Sign a document.

Questions 80 through 82 refer to the following telephone message.

Good afternoon, Darren. This is Olivia returning your call about the presentation I'll be giving at your company tomorrow. You asked if I need any special equipment or materials. I'm actually bringing all the materials with me. Equipment-wise, the only thing I'll really need is a video projector screen. Oh, and about your suggestion to pick me up from the airport, I already hired a limousine service, but thank you for the consideration nevertheless. See you tomorrow!

80. (   ) What is the speaker preparing to do?
  (A) Conduct a tour.
  (B) Organize a banquet.
  (C) Travel overseas.
  (D) Give a presentation.

81. (   ) What does the speaker request?
  (A) A copy of a contract.
  (B) Access to a network.
  (C) A list of guests.
  (D) A video screen.

82. (   ) Why does the speaker say, "I already hired a limousine service"?
  (A) To decline an offer.
  (B) To explain a procedure.
  (C) To request directions.
  (D) To propose a schedule change.

Here at Ridgemont Landscaping, we take safety very seriously, which is why we're holding this meeting today. Earlier this week, one of our installation sites was cited for multiple safety violations during a routine inspection. That is unacceptable. Let's begin by reviewing company safety policies. The binders on the table in front of you are yours to keep. They contain all our safety practices and they're divided into categories for your convenience. Unfortunately, I was pressed for time to get the materials together. I just noticed that some of the sections are out of order.

83. (   ) What kind of business do the listeners most likely work for?
   (A) A shoe manufacturer.
   (B) A landscaping firm.
   (C) A utility company.
   (D) A food and beverage distributor.

84. (   ) What is the purpose of the meeting?
   (A) To learn how to operate new equipment.
   (B) To discuss job openings.
   (C) To improve customer relations.
   (D) To review safety procedures.

85. (   ) Why does the man say, "I was pressed for time to get the materials together"?
   (A) To praise an employee.
   (B) To provide an excuse.
   (C) To accept an apology.
   (D) To change a deadline.

Questions 86 through 88 refer to the following telephone message.

Hi, this message is for Dylan Pietsch. My name is Susan and I'm one of the organizers of the Summer Music Festival. You recently sent us a registration form to reserve a booth at the fairgrounds. The problem is that it looks like you forgot to enclose the registration fee when you sent us the form. The fee is $250 per day and in order to be able to reserve a space for your company, we'll need the payment by next Friday. We're looking forward to having you there. It's going to be the biggest festival yet. Thousands of attendees have already registered and we're expecting many more to show up. Please call me back if you have any questions. Thanks.

GO ON TO THE NEXT PAGE.

86. (   ) What kind of event is the speaker organizing?
    (A) A fund-raising marathon.
    (B) An annual company outing.
    (C) A building dedication.
    (D) A music festival.

87. (   ) What is the speaker's reason for calling?
    (A) To explain a recent change in policy.
    (B) To confirm the number of attendees.
    (C) To discuss the content of a performance.
    (D) To request a missing payment.

88. (   ) What does the speaker say about the event?
    (A) The admission fee has increased.
    (B) There is limited seating.
    (C) It will be held at a different location.
    (D) It will be well-attended.

Questions 89 through 91 *refer to the following announcement.*

Thanks for being here this morning. As you know, the merger between Shipley Industries and DBK Supply was finalized this month. As a result of our companies joining forces, there's naturally going to be some restructuring of the organization, so I'm happy to announce that Norman Lee will be the new head of our industrial equipment division. We're very excited that he's taking on this role since he's an accomplished electrical engineer. His experience will be an asset in this position. Now, Norman is currently touring our factory in Oklahoma, but we expect him back here next Tuesday.

89. (   ) According to the speaker, what took place this month?
    (A) A department training.
    (B) A product launch.
    (C) A company merger.
    (D) A budget review.

90. (   ) What is Norman Lee's field of expertise?
    (A) Electrical engineering.
    (B) Graphic design.
    (C) Organic chemistry.
    (D) International law.

91. (   ) What is Norman Lee currently doing?
    (A) Developing a project budget.
    (B) Visiting a factory.
    (C) Conducting an experiment.
    (D) Meeting with the board of directors.

Questions 92 through 94 *refer to the following instructions.*

Welcome to our first Hatha yoga class here at the Shiva Wellness Center. I'm your instructor, Ines. To start, let me point out those lockers at the back of the room. You can use them to store your mats and workout attire for the entire course. Also, I know the classes are listed on the program as being from 11 a.m. to 1 p.m. However, we'll end 10 minutes early, so we'll have time to put the room back together. We share this space with a meditation class. Oh, and one more thing. Before you leave tonight, don't forget to stop by the registration desk to pay for the class if you haven't done so already.

92. (   ) What class does the speaker teach?
    (A) Graphic design.
    (B) Computer programming.
    (C) Martial arts.
    (D) Yoga.

93. (   ) Why does the speaker say, "We share this room with a meditation class"?
    (A) To invite students to another class.
    (B) To remind participants to watch their belongings.
    (C) To stress the importance of finishing on time.
    (D) To apologize for an inconvenient location.

94. (   ) What are the listeners reminded to do before they leave?
    (A) Replace their desks.
    (B) Pay for registration.
    (C) Take some handouts.
    (D) Provide some feedback.

GO ON TO THE NEXT PAGE.

Now for your KPRT local weather report. A storm passed through our city this morning, bringing much needed rain. Due to damage caused by the heavy winds earlier today, the traffic lights at the corner of Canfield Street and Swanson Avenue are not working. The traffic signals have been down for about an hour now and road crews have just started arriving to repair them. Officials report that the repairs should be finished by 6:00 p.m. and will not have any impact on tomorrow's 5K Run for Charity along Derby Street, so don't change your plans. We'll have more details about the race at the top of the hour.

95. (   ) What caused a problem?
    (A) Building demolition.
    (B) Bad weather.
    (C) A train delay.
    (D) An auto accident.

96. (   ) Look at the graphic. Which location is the speaker describing?
    (A) Location 1.
    (B) Location 2.
    (C) Location 3.
    (D) Location 4.

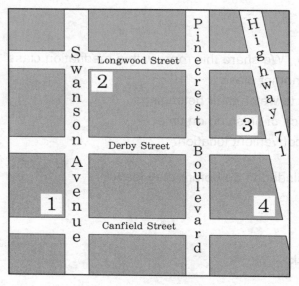

97. (   ) What does the speaker say will take place tomorrow?
    (A) A grand opening.
    (B) A race.
    (C) A parade.
    (D) A musical performance.

Questions 98 through 100 refer to the following talk and checklist.

Before we open the store today, let's go over our procedures for receiving book shipments. I'm concerned because a lot of time is wasted when these steps aren't followed. For example, sometimes cartons of books shipped from the company's warehouse are delivered to the wrong store. We don't want staff spending time inspecting merchandise that isn't meant for our store. So please pay attention to the store number the warehouse marks on each box. It must be the same as the number on the shipping invoice that's printed out daily. If not, we simply return the box unopened. It's important to remember this as we receive extra merchandise in preparation for the holiday season.

98. (   ) What does the speaker say he is concerned about?
    (A) Wasted staff time.
    (B) Customer complaints.
    (C) Excessive absences.
    (D) Limited storage space.

99. (   ) Look at the graphic. Which step does the speaker say requires special attention?
    (A) Step 1.
    (B) Step 2.
    (C) Step 3.
    (D) Step 4.

```
                Checklist

    1  _____
       Check store number

    2  _____
       Match titles with invoice

    3  _____
       Inspect books for damage

    4  _____
       Move items to storeroom
```

100. (   ) What does the speaker say is going to happen?
    (A) A sales event will begin.
    (B) A branch store will close.
    (C) Fewer shipments will be sent out.
    (D) More merchandise will arrive.

GO ON TO THE NEXT PAGE.

NO TEST MATERIAL ON THIS PAGE

New TOEIC Speaking Test

Question 1: Read a Text Aloud

 **Question 1**

Directions: In this part of the test, you will read aloud the text on the screen. You will have 45 seconds to prepare. Then you will have 45 seconds to read the text aloud.

Come to Middletown Autos, the area's most trusted used car dealer. Whether you're looking for a car, limo, truck, or van, we have a vehicle you'll love. Plus, we guarantee that the cars we sell are reliable and that our prices are reasonable. Thousands of customers have trusted us, so make sure that your next vehicle comes from Middletown Autos.

PREPARATION TIME
00 : 00 : 45

RESPONSE TIME
00 : 00 : 45

GO ON TO THE NEXT PAGE.

Question 2: Read a Text Aloud

 **Question 2**

Directions: In this part of the test, you will read aloud the text on the screen. You will have 45 seconds to prepare. Then you will have 45 seconds to read the text aloud.

Marketing strategy is a section of your business plan that outlines your overall game plan for how you'll find and attract clients or customers to your business. Sometimes marketing strategy is confused with a marketing plan, but they are different. Your marketing strategy focuses on what you want to achieve for your business and marketing efforts. A marketing plan details how you'll achieve those goals. A good marketing strategy incorporates what you know about how your business fits into the market and the marketing techniques and tactics that will achieve your marketing objectives.

PREPARATION TIME
00 : 00 : 45

RESPONSE TIME
00 : 00 : 45

Question 3: Describe a Picture

((◖ 5 ◗)) **Question 3**

Directions: In this part of the test, you will describe the picture on your screen in as much detail as you can. You will have 30 seconds to prepare your response. Then you will have 45 seconds to speak about the picture.

PREPARATION TIME
00 : 00 : 30

RESPONSE TIME
00 : 00 : 45

GO ON TO THE NEXT PAGE.

Question 3: Describe a Picture

答題範例

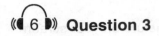 **Question 3**

Some men are standing in line.

They are probably trying to complete some kind of transaction.

It looks like a government office or public institution.

Most of the men are waiting to access window 13.

There's one man off to the side.

He's standing with his arms folded.

None of the other windows are open.

The line is cordoned off by some stanchions.

It's impossible to say if there are any workers behind the windows.

The man on the far left has a huge beer belly.

He's wearing glasses.

He's at the end of the line.

One of the men in line is wearing a cap.

The others have their backs to the camera.

There appears to be a person standing next to the man who is at
    window 13.

In the foreground, a couple of workers sit at desks.

They don't appear to be doing any work.

There's a bank of file cabinets on the left side.

Questions 4-6: Respond to Questions

 **Question 4**

Directions: In this part of the test, you will answer three questions. For each question, begin responding immediately after you hear a beep. No preparation time is provided. You will have 15 seconds to respond to Questions 4 and 5 and 30 seconds to respond to Question 6.

Imagine that a U.S. marketing firm is doing research in your country. You have agreed to participate in a telephone interview about public transportation.

Question 4

How often and for what purposes do you use public transportation?

Question 5

What is your experience with taxis and other types of car service?

Question 6

Describe one service or policy that you would like to be different about public transportation in your country.

GO ON TO THE NEXT PAGE.

Questions 4-6: Respond to Questions

答題範例

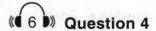 **Question 4**

How often and for what purposes do you use public transportation?

Answer

I use public transportation every day.

I take the bus to work.

Then I take the subway to visit my parents.

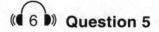 **Question 5**

What is your experience with taxis and other types of car service?

Answer

I use taxis occasionally.

There are times when I don't have a choice.

Taxis are expensive but otherwise quite helpful.

Questions 4-6: Respond to Questions

 **Question 6**

Describe one service or policy that you would like to be different about public transportation in your country.

Answer

> We have the Mass Rapid Transit (MRT) in Taipei.
>
> It's very efficient and dependable.
>
> It covers a lot of Taipei and New Taipei City.
>
> My only complaint is that it stops running at 12:20 AM.
>
> The local buses stop around the same time.
>
> Ending service at that hour is very inconvenient for me.
>
> Many people are still out in the city at that hour.
>
> We're either forced to go home early or take a taxi.
>
> Therefore, I wish the MRT ran 24 hours a day, 7 days a week.

GO ON TO THE NEXT PAGE.

Questions 7-9: Respond to Questions Using Information Provided

 Question 7

Directions: In this part of the test, you will answer three questions based on the information provided. You will have 30 seconds to read the information before the questions begin. For each question, begin responding immediately after you hear a beep. No additional preparation time is provided. You will have 15 seconds to respond to Questions 7 and 8 and 30 seconds to respond to Question 9.

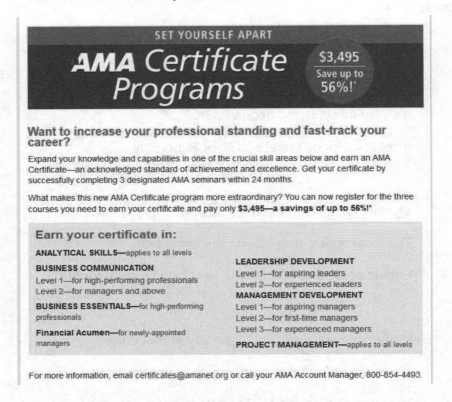

SET YOURSELF APART

AMA Certificate Programs

$3,495
Save up to 56%!'

Want to increase your professional standing and fast-track your career?

Expand your knowledge and capabilities in one of the crucial skill areas below and earn an AMA Certificate—an acknowledged standard of achievement and excellence. Get your certificate by successfully completing 3 designated AMA seminars within 24 months.

What makes this new AMA Certificate program more extraordinary? You can now register for the three courses you need to earn your certificate and pay only **$3,495—a savings of up to 56%!**

Earn your certificate in:

ANALYTICAL SKILLS—applies to all levels

BUSINESS COMMUNICATION
Level 1—for high-performing professionals
Level 2—for managers and above

BUSINESS ESSENTIALS—for high-performing professionals

Financial Acumen—for newly-appointed managers

LEADERSHIP DEVELOPMENT
Level 1—for aspiring leaders
Level 2—for experienced leaders
MANAGEMENT DEVELOPMENT
Level 1—for aspiring managers
Level 2—for first-time managers
Level 3—for experienced managers

PROJECT MANAGEMENT—applies to all levels

For more information, email certificates@amanet.org or call your AMA Account Manager, 800-854-4493.

Hi, I'm interested in the AMA Certificate Program. Would you mind if I asked a few questions?

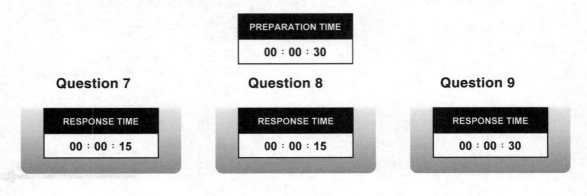

PREPARATION TIME
00 : 00 : 30

Question 7	Question 8	Question 9
RESPONSE TIME	RESPONSE TIME	RESPONSE TIME
00 : 00 : 15	00 : 00 : 15	00 : 00 : 30

Questions 7-9: Respond to Questions Using Information Provided

答題範例

 **Question 7**

How long does it take to earn a certificate?

Answer

> It varies from person to person.
>
> You must complete three courses within 24 months.
>
> Most people can finish the program in 12 months or less.

 Question 8

What makes this certificate program special?

Answer

> First of all, the certificate is a widely recognized standard
>
> of achievement.
>
> We're also running a promotional deal.
>
> Sign up now for three courses and save 56%.

GO ON TO THE NEXT PAGE.

Questions 7-9: Respond to Questions Using Information Provided

 **Question 9**

I'm interested in management development, but I don't have any experience.
Which level would be appropriate for me?

Answer

There are three levels of management development

courses.

Level three is for experienced managers.

Level two is for first-time managers.

Level one for people with no experience, like yourself.

However, you may plan on applying for a management

position in the near future.

Level one is the program for you.

Our certificate provides a solid management foundation.

You'll understand credibility and accountability.

You'll learn how to get things done.

Question 10: Propose a Solution

 **Question 10**

Directions: In this part of the test, you will be presented with a problem and asked to propose a solution. You will have 30 seconds to prepare. Then you will have 60 seconds to speak. In your response, be sure to show that you recognize the problem, and propose a way of dealing with the problem.

In your response, be sure to

- show that you recognize the caller's problem, and
- propose a way of dealing with the problem.

```
PREPARATION TIME
  00 : 00 : 30
```

```
RESPONSE TIME
  00 : 01 : 00
```

GO ON TO THE NEXT PAGE.

Question 10: Propose a Solution

答題範例

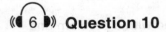 **Question 10**

Voice Message

Hey there, Michelle. This is George calling from Phoenix. Competition just wrapped up at the wrestling tournament here. Unfortunately, our flight home has been delayed. I'm really sorry, but this means I won't be able to make it to the regional athletic association meeting tomorrow. I know you were counting on me to represent our school at the meeting, and to vote for a new association chairperson. Do you think you could go in my place instead? On a positive note, I'm very pleased with how well our team did at the tournament. We had six wrestlers finish in the top three of their weight class. But I'll tell you all about it when I get back.

Question 10: Propose a Solution

答題範例

Hi George, I got your message.

Sorry to hear that you're stuck in Phoenix.

But I'm happy to hear the wrestling team did so well!

I could attend the meeting on your behalf.

I might be a little bit late, though.

I have to pick up my daughter from soccer practice.

However, I need some information from you first.

Who were you planning to vote for chairperson?

I'm not familiar with any of the candidates.

Maybe I should abstain from voting?

That's your call.

Let me know.

Anyway, great news about the team.

They represented our school well.

Please extend my congratulations.

Return my call when you can.

Travel safe.

Talk to you later.

GO ON TO THE NEXT PAGE.

Question 11: Express an Opinion

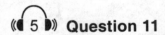 **Question 11**

Directions: In this part of the test, you will give your opinion about a specific topic. Be sure to say as much as you can in the time allowed. You will have 15 seconds to prepare. Then you will have 60 seconds to speak.

Some countries enforce the death penalty on their worst criminals.

Do you support the idea or oppose it? Give reasons to support your answer.

PREPARATION TIME
00 : 00 : 15

RESPONSE TIME
00 : 01 : 00

Question 11: Express an Opinion

答題範例

 **Question 11**

I fully support the idea.

The worst criminals should be put to death.

There is no reason to keep them alive.

The death penalty is based on the concept of deterrence of crime.

Criminals are deterred if the consequences of a crime outweigh the benefits.

Humans are basically aware of the differences between right and wrong.

The commission of crime is a free choice involving choices based on consequences of actions.

The death penalty is an effective deterrence to criminals.

The death penalty creates fear in the mind of potential offenders.

The death penalty eliminates villains and habitual killers from the society who would otherwise continue to harass people.

When a criminal is executed, he no longer poses any threat.

This follows the logical argument that the execution of killers and other radical offenders would contribute to safer societies.

Confining criminals to prisons and rehabilitation centers involves expenditure of taxpayer money.

The costs of a death penalty are low compared with the enormous expenditure of jail.

There are also arguments that if the criminals are released, it may lead to panic and fear in the society.

In addition, keeping criminals in prisons creates the possibility of escape from custody.

This means that the individuals could commit more crime.

The death penalty eliminates such possibilities of crime recurrence from the same criminal.

GO ON TO THE NEXT PAGE.

NO TEST MATERIAL ON THIS PAGE

New TOEIC Writing Test

Questions 1-5: Write a Sentence Based on a Picture

Question 1

Directions: Write ONE sentence based on the picture using the TWO words or phrases under it. You may change the forms of the words and you may use them in any order.

library / cart

答題範例：**The man is pushing a library cart.**

GO ON TO THE NEXT PAGE.

Questions 1-5: Write a Sentence Based on a Picture

Question 2

Directions: Write ONE sentence based on the picture using the TWO words or phrases under it. You may change the forms of the words and you may use them in any order.

writing / table

答題範例：**A woman is writing at a table.**

Questions 1-5: Write a Sentence Based on a Picture

Question 3

Directions: Write ONE sentence based on the picture using the TWO words or phrases under it. You may change the forms of the words and you may use them in any order.

player / judge

答題範例：**The player is complaining to the judge.**

GO ON TO THE NEXT PAGE.

Questions 1-5: Write a Sentence Based on a Picture

Question 4

Directions: Write ONE sentence based on the picture using the TWO words or phrases under it. You may change the forms of the words and you may use them in any order.

pour / coffee

答題範例：**The man is pouring some coffee.**

Questions 1-5: Write a Sentence Based on a Picture

Question 5

Directions: Write ONE sentence based on the picture using the TWO words or phrases under it. You may change the forms of the words and you may use them in any order.

man / shelf

答題範例：**The man is reaching for an item on a shelf.**

GO ON TO THE NEXT PAGE.

Questions 6-7: Respond to a written request

Question 6

Directions: Read the e-mail below.

From: karen@cohen-scott.com
To: admin@onwardandoutbound.com
Subject: Photo usage
Date: April 5

To Whom It May Concern,

My name is Karen Cohen-Scott, and I am an independent travel photographer who owns a set of photographs that were improperly posted on your travel blog, Outward & Outbound. While I noticed that I was properly credited as the photographer, your use of more than one image violates my policy posted at http://cohen-scott.com/usagepolicy. I am respectfully requesting you remove these images immediately.

However, I would be more than happy, for a fee, to provide photographs for your use.

Thank you,

Karen Cohen-Scott

Directions: Write back to Ms. Cohen-Scott as Reed Farber, owner of the travel blog. Apologize for the oversight and give ONE reason why you can't pay for the photographs.

Questions 6-7: Respond to a written request

答題範例

Question 6

Dear Ms. Cohen-Scott,

As owner of Outward & Outbound, I sincerely apologize for the improper use of your photographs on our travel blog. The photos have been removed and I pledge to be more careful in the future.

Outward & Outbound has been a Web presence for only two months and we've have been adding new content daily. Unfortunately, in our haste to launch our brand, we have made several errors. Apparently, we wrongly assumed that the author of said post had read your usage guidelines. Thus, we were not aware of your usage policies and licensing fee. I appreciate your patience with us regarding this incident and ask your forgiveness. When we saw your images we immediately recognized their exceptional quality. However, at this time we are unable to pay for content. I hope to purchase some of your work in the future when our website is better established and we have a budget for paid content.

Sincerely,
Reed Farber, Owner/Founder
Outward & Outbound

GO ON TO THE NEXT PAGE.

Questions 6-7: Respond to a written request

Question 7

Directions: Read the e-mail below.

From: Rodney Marchment
To: All Marchment Staff
Date: Thursday, July 23
Subject: Phone issues

To all supervisors and staff,

As you know, Marchment's is the most trusted name in electronics in the Sacramento area. However, our financial prospects continue to decline and it's time to shake things up. We have been in business for over 20 years. Just five years ago our annual sales were $75 million from our 12 stores, with two stores taking in over $15 million each. We all know that competition from big discount stores has severely cut into our sales. Consumers browse our merchandise but end up buying at the discount stores to save money. Even when we have major sales and match the discount retailers, people still buy from them. Last year's sales dropped to just $55 million dollars for our 8 remaining stores. If we can't reach sales of $60 million dollars before this year's end, we will be forced to close more locations. On the advice of my sister, an economist at Business Weekly, I am reaching out to all of you for feedback on how to increase sales and save our stores. Please e-mail me your ideas or call my secretary to arrange a meeting.

Thank you,

Stan Marchment
CEO
Marchment's Electronics

**Directions: Reply to Mr. Marchment as Robin Watson, a salesperson
with Marchment Electronics. List TWO problems and TWO
possible solutions.**

Questions 6-7: Respond to a written request

答題範例

Question 7

Mr. Marchment,

I have been with the company since the very beginning, and as salesperson in the stereo department, I too, have agonized over declining sales. I don't have a college degree but I realize that if we can't compete with discount stores, we will have to consolidate our operations. However, I can point to two areas of focus where we fail as a retailer. First, the big discounters have "no questions asked" return policies — and we don't. Sometimes people buy something, get it home, and it isn't what they wanted. Even my family buys from the discount stores for that reason alone. Second, we discontinued our used equipment program, which killed two birds with one stone. First, it allowed people to trade in and upgrade to a more expensive item. Second, people could buy equipment knowing they could return it for any reason. Thus, they were far more likely to make the initial purchase. Anyway, these are only my suggestions.

Sincerely,
Robin Watson
Stereo Dept.
10th Street Store

GO ON TO THE NEXT PAGE.

Questions 8: Write an opinion essay

Question 8

Directions: Read the question below. You have 30 minutes to plan, write, and revise your essay. Typically, an effective response will contain a minimum of 300 words.

It is sometimes said that borrowing money from a friend can harm or damage the friendship. Therefore, one must be careful when asking a friend for a loan. Write an essay in which you describe the best way to do this. Include specific details to explain your answer.

Questions 8: Write an opinion essay

答題範例

Question 8

Borrowing money from friends can be a slippery slope. It may completely change the relationship. There's a reason why today we still quote William Shakespeare's famous line from Hamlet, "Neither a borrower nor a lender be, for loan oft loses both itself and friend."

However, there are times when borrowing money from a friend is necessary and acceptable. First of all, you must have a solid relationship with the person. An acquaintance or someone you rarely speak to is not the best person to ask for a money loan. She or he should be a close, trustworthy friend with whom you would feel just as comfortable if the roles were reversed.

Next, be honest. If you're truthful about why you need the money, a friend will appreciate your openness and may be more inclined to help you. Also, don't be embarrassed to ask for advice. If you are asking a friend for money, you are assuming they have the funds to loan and most likely you see them as financially responsible. You may even ask your friend to look at your financial situation and help you create a budget. This gives your friend the assurance that you're not taking this request lightly.

Third, don't take your friend's generosity for granted. Even if your friend is known for being generous, you should never take advantage of that fact unless you're genuinely in a bind. You might consider putting your request in writing. State the amount you wish to borrow and the date you will pay the loan back. The loan should be taken seriously and tracked as if it were a loan from a bank. Keeping a good record will help prevent any resentment during the process.

Above all, you should only borrow money if you're confident you'll be able to pay the friend back—with interest, if necessary. It's crucial that you meet the terms of your verbal or written agreement. Do not go out and incur more debts or purchase things that may come across as wasteful expenditures in the eyes of your friend. With these guidelines in mind, you should be able to borrow money and still maintain a close friendship.

TOEIC 練習測驗 答案紙

LISTENING SECTION

Part 1

No.	ANSWER
1	Ⓐ Ⓑ Ⓒ Ⓓ
2	Ⓐ Ⓑ Ⓒ Ⓓ
3	Ⓐ Ⓑ Ⓒ Ⓓ
4	Ⓐ Ⓑ Ⓒ Ⓓ
5	Ⓐ Ⓑ Ⓒ Ⓓ
6	Ⓐ Ⓑ Ⓒ Ⓓ
7	Ⓐ Ⓑ Ⓒ Ⓓ
8	Ⓐ Ⓑ Ⓒ Ⓓ
9	Ⓐ Ⓑ Ⓒ Ⓓ
10	Ⓐ Ⓑ Ⓒ Ⓓ

Part 2

No.	ANSWER	No.	ANSWER
11	Ⓐ Ⓑ Ⓒ	21	Ⓐ Ⓑ Ⓒ
12	Ⓐ Ⓑ Ⓒ	22	Ⓐ Ⓑ Ⓒ
13	Ⓐ Ⓑ Ⓒ	23	Ⓐ Ⓑ Ⓒ
14	Ⓐ Ⓑ Ⓒ	24	Ⓐ Ⓑ Ⓒ
15	Ⓐ Ⓑ Ⓒ	25	Ⓐ Ⓑ Ⓒ
16	Ⓐ Ⓑ Ⓒ	26	Ⓐ Ⓑ Ⓒ
17	Ⓐ Ⓑ Ⓒ	27	Ⓐ Ⓑ Ⓒ
18	Ⓐ Ⓑ Ⓒ	28	Ⓐ Ⓑ Ⓒ
19	Ⓐ Ⓑ Ⓒ	29	Ⓐ Ⓑ Ⓒ
20	Ⓐ Ⓑ Ⓒ	30	Ⓐ Ⓑ Ⓒ

Part 3

No.	ANSWER	No.	ANSWER	No.	ANSWER
31	Ⓐ Ⓑ Ⓒ Ⓓ	41	Ⓐ Ⓑ Ⓒ Ⓓ	51	Ⓐ Ⓑ Ⓒ Ⓓ
32	Ⓐ Ⓑ Ⓒ Ⓓ	42	Ⓐ Ⓑ Ⓒ Ⓓ	52	Ⓐ Ⓑ Ⓒ Ⓓ
33	Ⓐ Ⓑ Ⓒ Ⓓ	43	Ⓐ Ⓑ Ⓒ Ⓓ	53	Ⓐ Ⓑ Ⓒ Ⓓ
34	Ⓐ Ⓑ Ⓒ Ⓓ	44	Ⓐ Ⓑ Ⓒ Ⓓ	54	Ⓐ Ⓑ Ⓒ Ⓓ
35	Ⓐ Ⓑ Ⓒ Ⓓ	45	Ⓐ Ⓑ Ⓒ Ⓓ	55	Ⓐ Ⓑ Ⓒ Ⓓ
36	Ⓐ Ⓑ Ⓒ Ⓓ	46	Ⓐ Ⓑ Ⓒ Ⓓ	56	Ⓐ Ⓑ Ⓒ Ⓓ
37	Ⓐ Ⓑ Ⓒ Ⓓ	47	Ⓐ Ⓑ Ⓒ Ⓓ	57	Ⓐ Ⓑ Ⓒ Ⓓ
38	Ⓐ Ⓑ Ⓒ Ⓓ	48	Ⓐ Ⓑ Ⓒ Ⓓ	58	Ⓐ Ⓑ Ⓒ Ⓓ
39	Ⓐ Ⓑ Ⓒ Ⓓ	49	Ⓐ Ⓑ Ⓒ Ⓓ	59	Ⓐ Ⓑ Ⓒ Ⓓ
40	Ⓐ Ⓑ Ⓒ Ⓓ	50	Ⓐ Ⓑ Ⓒ Ⓓ	60	Ⓐ Ⓑ Ⓒ Ⓓ

No.	ANSWER
61	Ⓐ Ⓑ Ⓒ Ⓓ
62	Ⓐ Ⓑ Ⓒ Ⓓ
63	Ⓐ Ⓑ Ⓒ Ⓓ
64	Ⓐ Ⓑ Ⓒ Ⓓ
65	Ⓐ Ⓑ Ⓒ Ⓓ
66	Ⓐ Ⓑ Ⓒ Ⓓ
67	Ⓐ Ⓑ Ⓒ Ⓓ
68	Ⓐ Ⓑ Ⓒ Ⓓ
69	Ⓐ Ⓑ Ⓒ Ⓓ
70	Ⓐ Ⓑ Ⓒ Ⓓ

Part 4

No.	ANSWER	No.	ANSWER	No.	ANSWER
71	Ⓐ Ⓑ Ⓒ Ⓓ	81	Ⓐ Ⓑ Ⓒ Ⓓ	91	Ⓐ Ⓑ Ⓒ Ⓓ
72	Ⓐ Ⓑ Ⓒ Ⓓ	82	Ⓐ Ⓑ Ⓒ Ⓓ	92	Ⓐ Ⓑ Ⓒ Ⓓ
73	Ⓐ Ⓑ Ⓒ Ⓓ	83	Ⓐ Ⓑ Ⓒ Ⓓ	93	Ⓐ Ⓑ Ⓒ Ⓓ
74	Ⓐ Ⓑ Ⓒ Ⓓ	84	Ⓐ Ⓑ Ⓒ Ⓓ	94	Ⓐ Ⓑ Ⓒ Ⓓ
75	Ⓐ Ⓑ Ⓒ Ⓓ	85	Ⓐ Ⓑ Ⓒ Ⓓ	95	Ⓐ Ⓑ Ⓒ Ⓓ
76	Ⓐ Ⓑ Ⓒ Ⓓ	86	Ⓐ Ⓑ Ⓒ Ⓓ	96	Ⓐ Ⓑ Ⓒ Ⓓ
77	Ⓐ Ⓑ Ⓒ Ⓓ	87	Ⓐ Ⓑ Ⓒ Ⓓ	97	Ⓐ Ⓑ Ⓒ Ⓓ
78	Ⓐ Ⓑ Ⓒ Ⓓ	88	Ⓐ Ⓑ Ⓒ Ⓓ	98	Ⓐ Ⓑ Ⓒ Ⓓ
79	Ⓐ Ⓑ Ⓒ Ⓓ	89	Ⓐ Ⓑ Ⓒ Ⓓ	99	Ⓐ Ⓑ Ⓒ Ⓓ
80	Ⓐ Ⓑ Ⓒ Ⓓ	90	Ⓐ Ⓑ Ⓒ Ⓓ	100	Ⓐ Ⓑ Ⓒ Ⓓ

READING SECTION

Part 5

No.	ANSWER	No.	ANSWER	No.	ANSWER
101	Ⓐ Ⓑ Ⓒ Ⓓ	111	Ⓐ Ⓑ Ⓒ Ⓓ	121	Ⓐ Ⓑ Ⓒ Ⓓ
102	Ⓐ Ⓑ Ⓒ Ⓓ	112	Ⓐ Ⓑ Ⓒ Ⓓ	122	Ⓐ Ⓑ Ⓒ Ⓓ
103	Ⓐ Ⓑ Ⓒ Ⓓ	113	Ⓐ Ⓑ Ⓒ Ⓓ	123	Ⓐ Ⓑ Ⓒ Ⓓ
104	Ⓐ Ⓑ Ⓒ Ⓓ	114	Ⓐ Ⓑ Ⓒ Ⓓ	124	Ⓐ Ⓑ Ⓒ Ⓓ
105	Ⓐ Ⓑ Ⓒ Ⓓ	115	Ⓐ Ⓑ Ⓒ Ⓓ	125	Ⓐ Ⓑ Ⓒ Ⓓ
106	Ⓐ Ⓑ Ⓒ Ⓓ	116	Ⓐ Ⓑ Ⓒ Ⓓ	126	Ⓐ Ⓑ Ⓒ Ⓓ
107	Ⓐ Ⓑ Ⓒ Ⓓ	117	Ⓐ Ⓑ Ⓒ Ⓓ	127	Ⓐ Ⓑ Ⓒ Ⓓ
108	Ⓐ Ⓑ Ⓒ Ⓓ	118	Ⓐ Ⓑ Ⓒ Ⓓ	128	Ⓐ Ⓑ Ⓒ Ⓓ
109	Ⓐ Ⓑ Ⓒ Ⓓ	119	Ⓐ Ⓑ Ⓒ Ⓓ	129	Ⓐ Ⓑ Ⓒ Ⓓ
110	Ⓐ Ⓑ Ⓒ Ⓓ	120	Ⓐ Ⓑ Ⓒ Ⓓ	130	Ⓐ Ⓑ Ⓒ Ⓓ

Part 6

No.	ANSWER	No.	ANSWER
131	Ⓐ Ⓑ Ⓒ Ⓓ	141	Ⓐ Ⓑ Ⓒ Ⓓ
132	Ⓐ Ⓑ Ⓒ Ⓓ	142	Ⓐ Ⓑ Ⓒ Ⓓ
133	Ⓐ Ⓑ Ⓒ Ⓓ	143	Ⓐ Ⓑ Ⓒ Ⓓ
134	Ⓐ Ⓑ Ⓒ Ⓓ	144	Ⓐ Ⓑ Ⓒ Ⓓ
135	Ⓐ Ⓑ Ⓒ Ⓓ	145	Ⓐ Ⓑ Ⓒ Ⓓ
136	Ⓐ Ⓑ Ⓒ Ⓓ	146	Ⓐ Ⓑ Ⓒ Ⓓ
137	Ⓐ Ⓑ Ⓒ Ⓓ		
138	Ⓐ Ⓑ Ⓒ Ⓓ		
139	Ⓐ Ⓑ Ⓒ Ⓓ		
140	Ⓐ Ⓑ Ⓒ Ⓓ		

Part 7

No.	ANSWER	No.	ANSWER	No.	ANSWER	No.	ANSWER	No.	ANSWER
147	Ⓐ Ⓑ Ⓒ Ⓓ	157	Ⓐ Ⓑ Ⓒ Ⓓ	167	Ⓐ Ⓑ Ⓒ Ⓓ	177	Ⓐ Ⓑ Ⓒ Ⓓ	187	Ⓐ Ⓑ Ⓒ Ⓓ
148	Ⓐ Ⓑ Ⓒ Ⓓ	158	Ⓐ Ⓑ Ⓒ Ⓓ	168	Ⓐ Ⓑ Ⓒ Ⓓ	178	Ⓐ Ⓑ Ⓒ Ⓓ	188	Ⓐ Ⓑ Ⓒ Ⓓ
149	Ⓐ Ⓑ Ⓒ Ⓓ	159	Ⓐ Ⓑ Ⓒ Ⓓ	169	Ⓐ Ⓑ Ⓒ Ⓓ	179	Ⓐ Ⓑ Ⓒ Ⓓ	189	Ⓐ Ⓑ Ⓒ Ⓓ
150	Ⓐ Ⓑ Ⓒ Ⓓ	160	Ⓐ Ⓑ Ⓒ Ⓓ	170	Ⓐ Ⓑ Ⓒ Ⓓ	180	Ⓐ Ⓑ Ⓒ Ⓓ	190	Ⓐ Ⓑ Ⓒ Ⓓ
151	Ⓐ Ⓑ Ⓒ Ⓓ	161	Ⓐ Ⓑ Ⓒ Ⓓ	171	Ⓐ Ⓑ Ⓒ Ⓓ	181	Ⓐ Ⓑ Ⓒ Ⓓ	191	Ⓐ Ⓑ Ⓒ Ⓓ
152	Ⓐ Ⓑ Ⓒ Ⓓ	162	Ⓐ Ⓑ Ⓒ Ⓓ	172	Ⓐ Ⓑ Ⓒ Ⓓ	182	Ⓐ Ⓑ Ⓒ Ⓓ	192	Ⓐ Ⓑ Ⓒ Ⓓ
153	Ⓐ Ⓑ Ⓒ Ⓓ	163	Ⓐ Ⓑ Ⓒ Ⓓ	173	Ⓐ Ⓑ Ⓒ Ⓓ	183	Ⓐ Ⓑ Ⓒ Ⓓ	193	Ⓐ Ⓑ Ⓒ Ⓓ
154	Ⓐ Ⓑ Ⓒ Ⓓ	164	Ⓐ Ⓑ Ⓒ Ⓓ	174	Ⓐ Ⓑ Ⓒ Ⓓ	184	Ⓐ Ⓑ Ⓒ Ⓓ	194	Ⓐ Ⓑ Ⓒ Ⓓ
155	Ⓐ Ⓑ Ⓒ Ⓓ	165	Ⓐ Ⓑ Ⓒ Ⓓ	175	Ⓐ Ⓑ Ⓒ Ⓓ	185	Ⓐ Ⓑ Ⓒ Ⓓ	195	Ⓐ Ⓑ Ⓒ Ⓓ
156	Ⓐ Ⓑ Ⓒ Ⓓ	166	Ⓐ Ⓑ Ⓒ Ⓓ	176	Ⓐ Ⓑ Ⓒ Ⓓ	186	Ⓐ Ⓑ Ⓒ Ⓓ	196	Ⓐ Ⓑ Ⓒ Ⓓ
								197	Ⓐ Ⓑ Ⓒ Ⓓ
								198	Ⓐ Ⓑ Ⓒ Ⓓ
								199	Ⓐ Ⓑ Ⓒ Ⓓ
								200	Ⓐ Ⓑ Ⓒ Ⓓ